COLTON

Sweet Southern Charmers Book 4

LORI WILDE &
CAROLYN GREENE

"**G**ive it to me, sweetie. Don't make me fight you for it." April Hanson crouched lower with her hand outstretched to the beautiful but goofy golden retriever.

Unfortunately, Maybelline had decided that a game of tag was in order. This happened every time she tried to teach the dog to fetch—only this time it was no newspaper they were battling over. The dog darted to one side, its rump stuck playfully in the air and a small gray object hanging from its mouth.

Straightening, April ran a hand through the blonde bangs that tickled her forehead. The direct approach obviously wouldn't work. But maybe she could distract Maybelline before the dog accidentally injured the baby squirrel she'd found.

Assuming a nonchalance she didn't feel, she strolled over to the base of the tree where the remains of the nest lay scattered on the ground. April guessed it had been ransacked by a hawk or an opossum.

She bent and picked up a burl from the ground. Maybelline's ears pricked forward in curiosity, and April teased the dog with the gnarled wood, holding it first behind her back, and then swinging it from side to side, just out of Maybelline's reach.

Just as she'd hoped, the retriever couldn't resist. When the small gray bundle dropped, forgotten, from the dog's mouth, April hurled the bit of wood as hard as she could into the thicket and made a move to run after it herself.

Sure enough, Maybelline rose to the challenge and went dashing off after it.

April gently picked up the young squirrel. Fortunately, it seemed unharmed by not only the nest marauder but Maybelline's teeth, as well. She cradled the squirrel to her chest in an attempt to warm it. The poor creature's eyes were not yet open, leading April to guess it was only about three or four weeks old.

"Poor sweet baby," she cooed. "You really got off to a rocky start, didn't you?"

Running a finger lightly over the tiny body, April hoped the squirrel hadn't been too stressed by the recent events in its short life. When it curled into a ball, April tucked the sleepy foundling down between her T-shirt and outer shirt. It squirmed until it found a comfy spot at her waist, then settled down for a nap. She would have to get little Rocky home soon and find him some milk.

April remounted her horse and placed a protective hand around the makeshift baby carrier. This was so typical of the way things turned out for her. She'd been wanting a baby of her own and look at what she ended up with. If that was how God answered prayers, then she supposed He must have a really whacked sense of humor.

On the ride back to the campground office, April quickly

finished her inspection, making note of fallen trees that needed to be cleared, as well as a blockage in the swollen stream that meandered its way to the man-made lake below.

Maybelline nosed in a pile of leaves, found a dried pinecone, and dashed away with the prize in her mouth. April touched her heels to the horse's ribs. The horse paused to nibble from a low-hanging branch.

"Come on, Daisy, let's go back to the stable and get some hay instead of those yucky dead leaves."

It was a beautiful spring morning. The Virginia weather had grown warm enough for shirtsleeves, and the trees had started budding, some of which burst forth with bright-green leaves.

The small bay mare, unable to contain her pent-up energy, stamped her hoof when April refused to loosen the reins for a gallop back to the stable.

When they neared the camp store, she noticed that the crocus bulbs she'd planted last fall had sprung up several inches in just a few days. A robin landed among the new shoots, snagged a blade of dry grass, and carried it off in its beak, presumably to line its nest.

"Good grief, it looks like the whole world is full of birth and new life."

Daisy's ears swiveled back at the brittle tone in her rider's voice.

"What are you looking so innocent for?" April asked. "I haven't forgotten how you decided to go gallivanting through the countryside, looking for a date. Old Man Grissom hasn't been the same since you stood outside his paddock, batting your eyelashes at his prize jumper stallion until Majesty's Thunder came over the fence after you."

The mare shook her mane, making it seem as though she was disagreeing with what April said.

"Knowing my luck, you're probably in foal and I'll have to pay a huge stud fee." Begrudgingly, she added, "At least you know how to pick 'em."

Unlike me, she added mentally and rubbed the tiny bundle at her waist. If she'd known how to pick a mate, she'd be married and have a houseful of snotty-nosed kids by now. April sighed.

What she wouldn't give to have a half dozen little noses, mouths, hands, and butts to wipe. Instead, at thirty-six, the sound of her biological clock was no longer just ticking but clanging away like crazy.

She loved the children she worked with as camp activity director, but April didn't know if she'd be able to take another season of watching parents flaunting their children. She knew they didn't actually *flaunt* them, but her long-unfulfilled desire to have a baby of her own made their teasing comments feel like a physical punch—right in the womb. "You want kids? Take mine." If only those people knew how much she wanted to take them up on their joking offers.

She rode up to the hitching post in front of the camp store, and her business partner stepped out onto the board planks.

Colton Radway stood there, looking at her ... *expectantly.*

Of course.

"What's the matter?" she asked.

"How about dinner and a movie tonight?" he suggested as he had every day for the past couple of years.

And just as she had done every day he asked that question, she ignored it. "No, really, what's wrong?"

"Nothing's wrong. Your niece called."

"Nicole? What did she want?"

Colton, her lifelong best friend and the man whom only she referred to as "Buddy," rocked back on his heels and rubbed the tension from his eyebrows. She'd seen that gesture a million times before, and usually it meant trouble.

"She didn't want anything. She has something to tell you." He reached into his back pocket and pulled out a cell phone.

"Oh, my gosh, something's wrong. I know it is."

He handed her the phone. "So, call her then."

"No."

She swung her leg over Daisy's neck. As she jumped down, Colton caught her waist, then cast a curious eye at the movement under her shirt.

"Squirrel," she said in explanation.

Obviously accustomed by now to the many orphaned creatures she brought back with her to mother, he didn't question further. He waited for her to take the cell phone.

Standing in front of him, closer now but still well below his eye level, April pushed the phone away. "The last two times Nicole called with something to tell me, she'd either eloped with that computer geek or been involved in a car accident."

Family members often said Nicole was enough like April to be her clone. So, it was no wonder that whenever her twenty-two-year-old niece got into trouble, she called her aunt to help her out of it.

"You know how I am with bad news," April told Colton. "Just tell me what she said so I can prepare for the worst."

Exasperated, Colton blurted, "You're going to be a great aunt. Okay?"

At April's strangled gasp, Daisy turned to look at her. April could have sworn the horse smiled.

Great aunt! She was too young to be a great aunt. Great aunts were always old, with gnarled, arthritic hands and thick bifocals. Just last year, April had to get glasses for the first time after she started having difficulty reading small print.

She looked down at her hands and studied the sprinkling of brown dots that she'd seen a million times and only just now really noticed. She'd always assumed they were freckles. But what if they were liver spots?

"Is something the matter?" Colton asked.

Of course, something was the matter. Her niece was pregnant, and *she* wasn't!

Colton pushed his ever-present Western hat back from his forehead and rubbed his eyebrows.

"I'm only thirty-six."

"True, but Nicole is a grown woman. Besides, she's married, so there's no reason to get upset."

The comment was a veiled reference to her mother's reaction to her sister's senior-year announcement that she was pregnant. The elder Hanson had reacted poorly to Stella's having a baby out of wedlock. Things hadn't changed much since then. Most of the folks in the small town of Bliss had similar traditional thoughts, and heaven help the person who failed to abide by their expectations.

"Yes, thank goodness she's married," April agreed. "Looks like Nicole managed to get John's mind off his computer—at least once."

Colton studied her for a moment, a concerned frown marring the handsome lines of his face. Then he put an arm around her shoulders. "He's not a bad guy, you know."

He was right. Perhaps her problem with John was jealousy. Nicole had someone with whom to start a family. And she didn't.

"Yeah, I suppose he'll be a good father." She looked up at Colton and smiled. "He'd *better* be a good father."

Colton smiled and handed her the phone. "Call Nicole. She can't wait to tell you the good news." He took Daisy's reins and turned to lead her back to the stable. Speaking over his shoulder, he added, "And try to sound like it's the first time you heard it."

April held the phone in her liver-spotted hands. Without her glasses, the numbers on the keypad were slightly blurred from this distance. She held the appliance at arm's length and squinted. There, that was better.

A sudden sense of panic came over April. If she was ever going to have a baby, she needed to do it now. If she waited any longer, she'd have gray hair by the time her child was ready to enroll in kindergarten.

This was ridiculous. First, she spent a couple of years married to the wrong man. Then she spent several more years looking for the right man who, by the way, never showed up. After that, she devoted most of her energy to working with Colton to turn the campground into a profit maker.

As the years slowly slipped away, so did her opportunities for finding a good husband and father. Most of the men in her age range were either firmly married or entering their midlife crises and looking for women at least ten years younger than April. With each passing year, the slim pickings became even more meager.

A growing plume of dust in the distance caught her attention. Down the graveled road that led into the campground, a small dot of a car approached. Probably a family coming for an early-in-the-season weekend camping trip. She hoped they didn't have a baby or toddler with them.

The coming summer months would only bring more babies, toddlers, and elementary school-age children to their campground, and she would be responsible for keeping them entertained with age-appropriate activities. She knew she couldn't take another season of coveting other people's children.

She closed the cover on the phone. She would call her

niece after she got this family settled into a campsite. And even if she had to grit her teeth while doing it, she would sound happy for Nicole.

Watching the dust plume come closer, April felt her spirits lift as soon as she settled upon a course of action. *There's no time like the present,* Colton always said.

Little Rocky wiggled at her waist as if to reinforce the thought that had entered her head.

She was going to have a baby no matter what it took. A smile formed on her lips, and relief settled over her heart at the decision she'd made. Making up her mind was the easy part. The true test of character would be following through with the plan.

The car pulled into the parking lot, but this was no family to torment her with a car full of adorable children. It was one of the sheriff's department vehicles.

The deputy got out, stretched, and took a leisurely look around.

"The camping season has hardly started," April said. "Surely Mrs. Turner doesn't have anything to complain about already."

The man closed the car door and pocketed the key. Stepping forward with a swagger that seemed forced on someone of his short stature, he hooked his thumbs through his belt loops and smiled. The weekend deputy's name badge, obviously carefully polished, winked at her in the sunlight. Dugg, it read. She'd heard he was a salesclerk at Reece Masardi's feed and seed store Monday through Friday. His part-time job, however, was what he lived for.

"It's not your campers that's bothering Mrs. Turner this time," he drawled. "I understand you have a young hoodlum working for you now."

"Steven is a kid who's trying to turn his life around. I

won't have anyone, including you, referring to him in that manner."

As he drew himself up and squared his shoulders, April could tell she'd made a mistake. Despite his effort at appearing more authoritative, her riding boots gave her an inch on him in height. That and her statement served to undermine the tenuous hold he had on the respect he seemed to crave. But right now, April didn't care about his personal agenda. She was more concerned about Steven.

Dugg had been a repeat visitor to their campground ever since the elderly Bea Turner had moved into the house at the near corner of the campground last summer. He seemed to relish the "showdown" between the two neighbors and gleefully issued repeated warnings and citations. A couple of times she and Colton had had to appear in court for disturbing the peace, all because of the dance contests she staged for the teenagers each Friday night during their busy season. The music was always silenced by eleven o'clock, but that never stopped the determined deputy from writing up yet another darned citation.

The woman had not stopped complaining since she'd moved in. There had been letters to the editor of the local newspaper, griping to other residents, and even an attempt to raise a petition against the campground's "noisy activities."

Fortunately, no one other than Mrs. Turner had a complaint against them. But she was still managing to make life difficult for them.

Since most of their activities took place on the weekends, they'd come to know the over enthusiastic Alexander Dugg better than they would have liked.

Colton returned from the barn and stood beside April in a show of solidarity. The twitching muscle in his jaw was his only outward sign of annoyance. His voice came out in a deep rumble. "Is there a problem, Deputy Dugg?"

April almost smiled as her partner slurred the last two words until they sounded like the name of an old-time cartoon dog. There was no mistaking he'd done it intentionally.

"It seems as though that reform school dropout of yours was loitering behind your neighbor's shed yesterday. And now she's missing some tools that she stored out there." He paused, then added in a serious tone, "They belonged to her late husband."

April's humor disappeared at the allegation leveled against the teen Colton had taken under his wing. Initially, he'd been against having a boy from the juvenile corrections facility working for them. But after he'd come to know Steven, he came to see he'd been wrong in assuming the worst about him.

"Steven works hard here," she said. "He doesn't have the time or the desire to get into trouble."

The boy *had* been on that section of the campground property yesterday, repairing loose boards and pounding nails that had worked their way out of the salt-treated wood fence. But April had no doubt that he'd stayed on campground property. He was trying hard to prove himself to Colton. The teen wouldn't throw it away by doing something as foolish as what the deputy was implying.

Colton straightened the tall brown hat that often served as an indicator of his moods. Today, perched menacingly low over his scowling brow, it sent a clear warning. He frowned at Dugg.

"Are you here to press charges?"

"No, no," Dugg insisted, waving his hands. "There isn't enough evidence. But I *am* here to issue a warning. Perhaps you could hint to the boy that if those tools are mysteriously returned to Mrs. Turner—undamaged—then we'll forget about the whole incident. Provided, of course, no other items disappear from her property in the future."

April was about to tell him what he could do with those tools, but Colton placed a firm hand on her shoulder. When she opened her mouth to speak, he quelled her protest with a slight shake of his head.

She supposed he was right. Dugg's citation pad had stayed in his pocket on this particular visit. If she started arguing with him now, he'd surely charge them with some infraction —real or imagined—that he could think of on the spot.

Colton turned to go inside and paused at the door to the building that served as a combination camp store and recreation room.

"We'll mention to Steven about Mrs. Turner's missing tools, but I'm certain he doesn't know anything about them." Holding the door for April, he added, more for Dugg's ears than hers, "There's too much work to do for us to be standing around out here."

Without so much as a word of goodbye, he ushered her inside and followed with a firm click of the door. To their surprise, the bell above the door tinkled again as it swung open and their nemesis stepped inside.

Clyde, their part-time employee, wheeled his chair out from the aisle where he'd been stocking pool toys in preparation for the summer guests. When he saw who was with them, he reversed the direction of his wheelchair.

"Is there something else?" Colton delivered the words more as a statement of dismissal than a question.

The deputy paced down the aisle where Clyde was now loading shelves with plastic snorkels and inflatable pool toys. He examined the procedure as if he were about to give the elderly gentleman a performance review.

Turning back to Colton, he asked, "Got any cold drinks?"

Colton's hat brim nodded toward the refrigerated

compartment along the back wall where large red lettering above it spelled out COLD DRINKS.

The deputy went to the cooler, retrieved an orange soda, and downed half of it before he reached into his pocket to pay for it. He was headed toward the cash register when he abruptly stopped, peered through the refrigerator's glass doors, and studied the neat rows of bottles, cans, and cartons. The pink-faced man grinned as if he'd single-handedly tracked and apprehended one of America's most wanted criminals.

Alexander Dugg licked his lips and hitched his breeches a little higher.

"What do we have here?" Dugg asked, reaching once again into the cooler.

April's stomach felt as though it hit the floor. It was clear Colton had also seen the can of beer in Dugg's hand.

From Dugg's smug smile, April supposed he was picturing the headline: *Deputy Busts Campground Owners for Illegal Alcohol Sales*. Perhaps he even imagined that Lisa LaQuinta, the TV news reporter, would interview him. If April knew Dugg as well as she thought, he was probably making a mental note to take his uniform to the cleaners for the occasion. And he'd ask for extra starch. She wouldn't be surprised if he thought such publicity would give him a shot at the sheriff's job in the next election.

The deputy sauntered to the front of the building and placed the can on the counter in front of April. "How much do you charge for this?"

"We don't," April said. Remembering the deputy's eagerness to achieve his self-made quota each weekend, she forced herself to speak with as much caution as she could muster. "We don't sell alcohol here."

"Coulda fooled me." Dugg turned the can over to display the price tag. "Let me see your liquor license."

When Colton stepped forward, Dugg touched the gun at his side as if to reassure himself it was still there.

Apparently noticing the deputy's find, Clyde rolled his chair toward them and cleared his throat to say something. The expression of guilt on his face made him look, despite his seventy-plus years, like a small boy holding a baseball bat near a broken window.

She should have known. Clyde had often remarked that he slept better at night after "downing a cold one." But she didn't realize he'd been keeping those beers in the camp store's cooler.

Before he could speak, however, Colton silenced him with a slight shake of the head. "That's mine," he told Dugg. "It's for personal use."

To make sure their employee didn't make matters worse by confessing his part in the mix-up, April distracted him by handing him the squirrel to care for. For a moment Clyde looked torn between responsibilities, but ultimately went away to look for a box and bedding for his new charge.

"Personal use, my eye," the deputy argued. "This can has a *price sticker* on it."

Colton's hands moved to his blue-jeaned hips. With his feet slightly apart, ready for confrontation, he reminded April of a cowboy preparing to shoot it out.

"If you'll take a look around," he said, his voice low and steady, "you'll see that we don't sticker any of our drinks. The price list is posted on the cooler door."

Her partner's patience was being tested, perhaps more than her own. It was stupid, having to put up with this kind of harassment, but there came a point when it was senseless to fight over inanities. Maybe if they just took their lumps and made an appropriate apology, the deputy would go away satisfied that he'd won.

"Look," said April, "we have a business to run, and I'm

sure you have some other deputying to do. So why don't you just tell us how much we owe, and we can call an end to this misunderstanding."

She pulled her purse out from under the counter. Colton tried to stop her, but it was too late. Her wallet was already open, and she was counting out bills onto the Formica counter. A low moan escaped the back of his throat.

Dugg's eyes widened. "Miz Hanson, you are obviously mistaken about my ethics as a law enforcer."

A quizzical expression crossed her face. "What? I only—"

If he let her say anything else, she was only going to worsen the situation. Colton spoke up, effectively preventing her from digging the hole any deeper. "I believe my partner is trying to say that she would be willing to pay whatever *fine* is involved."

But Dugg wouldn't accept his explanation. "I'm going to have to charge you both with selling beer without a license." He glanced at April. "And attempting to bribe an officer of the law."

She tried to protest but was drowned out as Dugg launched into the Miranda speech. "You have the right to remain silent..." When he finished reading them their rights, he fished a pair of handcuffs out of his back pocket.

Clyde rolled his chair toward them, the squirrel in a cardboard box on his lap, and rubbed the sprinkling of gray whisker stubs on his chin. "Colton, I gotta tell you—"

Colton cut him off. "We need you to stay here and take care of things until we get back. And keep an eye out for Steven. He should be arriving soon."

His message was clear. Don't say anything else, or there will be three of us going to the sheriff's office.

"Hold out your wrists," Dugg said to April.

She stared helplessly at the cuffs the little man held out

toward her. With a quick, pleading glance at Colton, she slowly lifted her arms.

A knot formed in Colton's gut. There was no way he was going to stand by and let that little twerp handcuff April. His big hand shot out and, without thinking about the consequences, he snatched the metal hardware from the deputy. "Hey!" Dugg yelped. "Give those back."

"You are not going to put these things on her."

"Okay, you've done it now." Dugg hitched his pants up and touched the gun at his side. "I'm going to have to charge you with interfering with an officer of the law in the performance of his duties."

This wasn't Mayberry, and Colton doubted the deputy was required to carry his bullets in his shirt pocket. Since Dugg was already agitated and obviously out of control of the situation, Colton knew it would be foolhardy to back him into a corner.

"Charge me as you see fit," he said, dangling the stainless-steel cuffs from one finger, "but the lady doesn't wear this style of bracelet."

Dugg grabbed the cuffs from Colton and stepped back a pace as though he might get bitten if he ventured too close. "I'm gonna have to ask you to hold out your arms."

April moved beside him, and Colton felt her arm slip around his waist. "You don't need to use those on him," she said. "He's never hurt anyone in his life."

If the deputy hadn't been clamping steel around his right arm, Colton would have smiled at her words. She'd conveniently forgotten about the times he'd defended her from schoolyard bullies and left them with bruises or bloodied noses.

He waited patiently for the circle to close around his left arm, but Dugg said, "*Behind* your back."

"Oh, for crying out loud!" April stepped away as Colton turned to accommodate the deputy.

Their eyes met, and Colton wished he could protect her as easily now as when they were kids.

~

The cell door opened, and April entered looking as repulsed as she had when the door had first been opened to them more than an hour ago.

Was Nicole home?

Colton slid to one side of the narrow bench attached to the cinder block wall. She looked so pathetic it was all he could do to keep from taking her in his arms and holding her. After all, they had an agreement. Well, they didn't, but he let her *think* they did.

Shortly after he'd returned to Bliss County to start running Cozy Acres Family Campground with her, he'd suggested they go out together. April was quick to remind him they were friends and business partners first and foremost. She didn't want to mess up their friendship like she'd done with her ex-husband.

Damn that Eddie for everything he'd done.

April might consider him her best buddy, but Colton wanted more than a "just friends" relationship with her. Just as water wore down rocks in the creek bed, he would wear down her resistance. Somehow, he would find a way to make her stop seeing him as a friend and start seeing him as a potential lover.

She sat next to him. Following his earlier impulse, Colton put an arm around her and tugged her to him. To his surprise and pleasure, she didn't resist but leaned against him and sighed heavily.

"Nicole will be here in about twenty minutes," she said.

"Thank goodness she was home. If Mom finds out about this, I'll never hear the end of it."

Considering that Mrs. Hanson still lamented her older daughter's indiscretion of getting pregnant while unmarried and in high school, he had no doubt April would receive an ear bending for this brush with the law.

And calling her niece to come pick them up wouldn't keep the news from April's mother. In a town the size of Bliss, there was no doubt the elder Hanson would learn of it eventually.

A wayward fluff of April's blonde hair caressed the pulse point of his neck. He chuckled, as much from being tickled as from what she said. "That's a switch, Nicole bailing *you* out for a change."

She stared, dead-eyed, at the cell door.

"She told you her news?"

April glanced up and gave him a small smile. "I acted surprised."

Their physical closeness was making him restless. Colton stood and paced the small enclosure they shared. Apparently, Deputy Dugg, or others like him, had been busy today, which made for a full house.

The cinder block walls between cells afforded a small amount of privacy unless the neighboring jailbird was industrious and more than a little curious. In one smooth movement, Colton stepped to the bars at the front of the cell and confiscated a pocket-sized mirror from the hand that had reached around the corner.

"Hey, man, I was just checking out the babe!" a male voice protested. "Ask her if she wants to go dancing."

"She's not interested," Colton growled.

"Tell her I got all my teeth."

Colton shoved the mirror into his pocket and turned to see April's reaction. But instead of responding to their neighbor's dental condition, she quietly announced, "Liver spots or not, I'm going to have a baby."

He stopped in his tracks. He didn't know what she meant by the first part of her statement, but the last part felt like a kick in the gut with steel-toed boots. What was a guy supposed to say when the woman he cared about—the only woman he'd ever cared about—said she was pregnant with another man's baby? *If it's a boy, name it after me?* He hadn't even realized she was seeing anyone.

"I'm going to kill the guy," he muttered.

2

April lifted her chin from her hands. "What?"

He wasn't up on the etiquette. Was he supposed to congratulate her or offer his sympathy? Or maybe he should suggest she have an ambulance standing by when she told her mother, because the news that her "good daughter" was pregnant was certain to send Mrs. Hanson into cardiac arrest.

Instead, he blurted the first thing that came to his mind. "Who's the father?"

"The father?"

"Yes, the last I heard it takes two to make a baby." There was an edge to his voice, but he couldn't help himself. Still, her expression was enough to make him clamp his teeth together to prevent another outburst. She'd always confided in him, and even though he didn't like what he'd just heard, he didn't want her to shut him out.

"I—I don't know," she said, getting up from the bench. "Not yet."

Despite his resolve to temper his comments, Colton couldn't hold back. "You don't know?"

Panic set in as he considered the possibility that she hadn't been careful about her partners or, more importantly, her health.

Her back was to him. Gripping her shoulders, he turned her around. Her short blond hair swung about her face. "You don't know?" he repeated.

"I'll find out," she said with conviction. "It's not like I won't know his hair color or whether he's tall or short. And I'm sure he's very bright." She squirmed under his hands. "You're hurting my shoulders."

Colton released her and shoved his hands into his back pockets to keep them still. It didn't take a bright man to see how attractive she was and take advantage of her trust. And apparently, she'd been *very* trusting. His hands came out of his pockets as he punctuated the air with them.

"You mean you won't know until the baby is born? And have you forgotten there are diseases out there?"

"Relax, Buddy," April said as if she were instructing a new rider on how to sit a saddle. "The fertility clinic checks the donors before they, um, contribute."

Colton frowned. "Fertility clinic?"

"Yeah, the one in Richmond, near Arthur Ashe Boulevard."

"You don't need no fertility clinic," the voice called from the adjoining cell. "I got real strong swimmers."

"You mean, you're not pregnant now?" Colton demanded.

"Why, do you think I look fat?"

Colton began pacing again. How could she think of doing such a thing? "You can't go down to the clinic."

April opened her mouth, then promptly closed it and plopped herself down onto the bench. She stared up at him for a moment before responding.

"I'm almost thirty-seven years old, Buddy, and I'm not

getting any younger. If I'm ever going to have a baby, now's the time to do it." She folded her arms across the *Just Do It* slogan on her shirt.

"Maybe if you thought it over some more—"

"This is not a whim. It's not a decision I came to lightly." She reached down and picked up the cowboy hat he'd set on the bench earlier. Smoothing the band around the weathered crown, she added, "You don't have to agree with what I'm doing, but I would appreciate it if you were supportive of my decision."

How could he support her getting pregnant with another man's child, no matter how anonymous the donor might be?

"What about the baby?" he asked. "Do you think it's fair to raise a kid without a father?"

"After the divorce, my mother raised my sister and me all by herself, and we turned out okay."

Colton grew silent. Stella, her older sister, had become pregnant in her senior year of high school. Had she been looking for the male affection that she no longer got from her absentee father?

As for April, she'd impulsively married their mutual friend Eddie Brock the semester after Colton went away to college. Perhaps she'd been searching for the happiness and companionship that was so obviously lacking in her mother's life.

Though April had a reputation for being impulsive, and he had the habit of bailing her out of her mishaps, he felt certain she'd given a lot of thought to her decision to have a baby.

She'd be a good mother, that's for sure. All anyone had to do was watch her with the kids at the campground to see how much she loved them. And they all returned her affection, some of the younger ones crying when their vacation was over and they had to leave "Miss April." Nevertheless, Colton worried that she was letting her heart rule her head once again. When she did that, all he could do was go along, try to protect her as best he could, and hope for the best.

"That clinic is in a bad part of town," he declared. "I'll take you there."

In the next moment, a uniformed officer turned a key in the lock, and the barred door swung open. "You're free to go," he said.

As they left to join Nicole, the man in the next cell called out, "Goodbye, pretty lady. It would have been nice knowing you."

"I didn't do anything, Colton. I swear I didn't." Steven's voice cracked, and he hoped his boss wouldn't mistake the changing of his hormones for guilt. The teenager glanced from Colton to April, silently beseeching them to believe him.

Bea Turner got off her golf cart and tottered up to the camp store porch. Colton was immediately beside her, offering an arm in assistance up the step, but the elderly woman waved him off.

"There's no need to hover," she snapped. "I'm not going to fall on your property and sue you."

Steven could tell April and Colton hadn't considered that possibility. Even so, he knew they would refuse to think the worst, believing that everything would soon be worked out to everyone's satisfaction. He wasn't so sure.

"What seems to be missing this time, Mrs. Turner?" April gestured in invitation toward the empty bench, but their neighbor shook her head and clutched her black handbag tighter under her arm.

"Someone came into my yard and took some of my crafting supplies." Steven caught the significant look she threw him before continuing. "I had been crocheting a *Gone with the Wind* doll for my sister Marlene's granddaughter. That dear girl loves the color blue, don't you know, so I was using a variegated blue yarn for Scarlett's dress and hat. Got it on sale at Walmart the last time Marlene drove me to town."

Steven shoved his hands into his pockets, wishing she'd get to the point so he could prove his innocence and get back to work. April and Colton merely exchanged patient glances, which Mrs. Turner obviously interpreted as curiosity about her shopping habits.

"She comes for me every so often," she explained, "and we go shopping and have lunch at the cafeteria. Sometimes we even go over to the flea market, but you gotta be careful when you buy stuff there because they'll call old junk an antique and try to charge you more than it's worth."

Steven shifted beside April. "What's that got to do with—"

April whacked him with her elbow, and while he rubbed his ribs, she asked politely, "What about your doll, Mrs. Turner?"

The older woman adjusted her blue-rimmed glasses and stared through them at Steven. "Well, I went into the house for a glass of iced tea, and it took a few minutes longer than I expected. I'd forgotten to add the sugar after I brewed it the day before, so the sugar wouldn't melt, what with all the ice in it. And I despise that artificial sweetener which Marlene says melts faster, but I wouldn't know because I don't use it."

This time Colton shifted as he pushed his ever-present hat off his forehead and rubbed his eyebrows. "And when you came back outside..." he prompted.

Mrs. Turner straightened her small body and placed a hand on her well-rounded hip. "If you'll refrain from interrupting, young man, I'll finish telling you what happened."

Steven didn't have to look at his employer to know that

his expression never changed from respectful concern. He wished he had Colton's restraint. If it weren't for the seriousness of the accusation against Steven, it would be all he could do to keep from laughing at the old broad's craziness.

"And when I came back a few minutes later," Mrs. Turner proceeded, "the doll form was missing. The yarn and dress I'd started were still there, but the plastic doll was gone."

It was such a stupid thing to make such a fuss over. But April was a peacemaker, even when it came to her crotchety neighbor. Steven scratched his chin as she tried to humor the old lady. "Are you sure it didn't fall to the ground when you got up to go inside?"

"*Everything* was topsy-turvy on the ground when I returned," Mrs. Turner said. "Even my lawn chair. The only thing that wasn't on the ground was the doll. And it wasn't there because it had been *stolen*," she declared, jabbing her pocketbook in Steven's direction. "He must have knocked the chair over in his hurry to get away."

Steven opened his mouth in horrified indignation. It was bad enough being accused of theft, but even worse to be accused of stealing a doll. "What would I want with her stupid old—"

Once again April's elbow found a home against his ribs. Pressing a hand to his side, he wisely chose not to finish his sentence.

He would have liked to tell the crazy woman what she could do with her doll, but it was just as well that April answered for him. "What he meant to say, Mrs. Turner, is that boys his age don't play with dolls, so he had no reason to take it."

Mrs. Turner made a noise, *pshaw*-ing her statement. "She's naked!"

If Steven and Colton had been canines, their ears would have stood straight up.

"Who's naked?" Steven blurted, looking around him. Although it was obvious that Colton tried not to show it, his eyes were also peeled in preparation for an unexpected visual treat. If this was one of those male bonding moments his youth counselor had told him about, then Steven was all for it.

"Why, Scarlett, of course." Mrs. Turner lowered her voice and leaned toward April. "I know how a teenage boy's mind works."

Right now, his mind was telling him to throw up.

Steven could tell Colton was trying to keep a straight face. His mentor moved to the porch rail and rested his back pockets against it. "It seems to me that if a boy wanted to look at the female form, he wouldn't need a toy to peek at. He could see the real thing on many television shows. Or the internet."

Obviously, their neighbor was not appeased by their attempts to explain away the missing doll. Mrs. Turner clutched her purse to her bosom and gingerly lowered herself down the single step from the porch to the grass-grown parking lot when April made another attempt to set things straight.

"I have to go into town to buy some things for a family reunion," April said. "I'd be happy to pick up a new doll and some yarn while I'm there."

"I don't want your charity. I want the one who's been stealing my stuff to return it and to apologize in person." Mrs. Turner climbed onto the golf cart seat. "I should have known you two would take his side. I suppose I'll have to call the youth facility myself and report what's been happening since that boy came to work here."

The golf cart cranked to life, and Mrs. Turner puttered away without another word, the wind whipping her flowered jersey skirt to expose knee-high stockings that ineffectually camouflaged the varicose veins snaking across her calves.

Steven and Colton noticed the fist-size rock in the driveway at the same time. Colton's voice was quiet but deep with authority. "Don't even *think* it."

Steven clenched his hands. Getting a job here at Cozy Acres with Colton and April was one of the best things that had ever happened to him. And now the old lady was threatening to mess everything up.

April watched as emotions flickered across the boy's face. Then, resignedly, Steven slid his hands into his pockets, clenched his teeth, and hissed something that sounded like "witch."

She hated to bring it up, hated that she was being forced into what might seem like an act of betrayal against the boy she'd grown so fond of these past few months. "You know we're going to have to tell your youth counselor about this."

He kicked the rock he'd been eyeing earlier.

April glanced at Colton, silently pleading for him to back her up. He hadn't wanted Steven here in the first place. He had worried that the benefits of helping a kid who'd been in trouble with the law would be outweighed by the problems associated with helping him. She hoped he wouldn't say "I told you so" in front of Steven.

Maybe Colton was right when he had argued against having the teen work with them. Maybe she should have found another outlet for her mother hen urges. Even so, she believed in Steven. Mrs. Turner didn't know him like she did. Didn't know how hard he worked, even when he wasn't aware of being watched. After some bumpy episodes the first few weeks, his anger had softened, and he seemed to be trying to please them with his promptness and by working as hard as a man twice his size. April hoped this episode with Mrs. Turner wouldn't cause them to lose the ground they'd gained with Steven.

Colton spoke so softly April could barely hear him. "It's better that your counselor hears it first from us."

Although Steven was clearly agitated, he didn't argue with Colton. But his knuckles whitened as he repeatedly clenched and relaxed his fingers.

"The stalls need to be mucked," Colton told him. "Why don't you work off some of that steam while we try to get this mess straightened out."

It was a job Steven normally detested, but he jogged off toward the barn without a word of protest.

April glanced up at Colton, grateful for his part in mentoring Steven, not just today but every day. She could have said the very same words or shown more compassion, but for some reason known only to teenage boys, the effect wouldn't have been the same. "I hope he doesn't take his anger out on the horses."

"He'll be fine. I'm more concerned about him taking his anger out on Mrs. Turner." Colton turned to go inside. "Let's keep a close eye on him these next few days and don't assign him any work near her property."

It was several days before April could get an appointment with the fertility specialist. She'd tried to talk Colton out of going with her, insisting she could take care of herself, but he wouldn't hear of it.

They fought the downtown traffic before finding the building next to an ancient townhouse that was being refurbished. The block held an assortment of houses, some of which had been converted to offices, all with neatly trimmed postage-stamp lawns. "This doesn't look like such a bad neighborhood," April observed.

Colton reached for the gearshift and maneuvered into the opening at the curb. "This section is being revitalized, but two blocks over, the houses are run down and not far from there it can be dangerous. Just last week, there were two shootings."

April shivered despite the warmth of the spring day.

"Makes me glad I live in Bliss. It's a good place to raise a family."

Colton came around and opened the car door for her. "Yeah, it's too bad your family won't be complete."

"What's that supposed to mean?"

They walked past a row of purple pansies that lined the sidewalk to the clinic.

"It means, what are you going to do when your kid asks about his dad? Show him a picture of a test tube?"

He had opened the glass-paned door and was holding it for her, but she stopped and stared at her lifelong best friend. "I thought you understood why I'm doing this," she said, more than a little hurt by his lack of support.

"Just because I understand it doesn't mean I agree with it. I just happen to think that a kid should grow up with *both* parents, like I did."

"Well, for your information, Colton Michael Radway, not everyone is as fortunate as you are." April placed a hand on her hip and tried to stare him down, which was hard to do, considering he was at least six inches taller than she. "If you can't be happy that I'm finally going to have what I've always wanted, then you can just leave right now. I won't have you spoiling what could be the happiest event of my life."

He'd known her long enough to realize there was no arguing with her when she was like this. Shoot, he'd been trying for years to convince her to go out with him, to no avail.

She had some cockamamie idea in her head that her first marriage didn't work out because she'd married a friend, which was why she turned down his daily date invitations. Still, he couldn't help driving home his point.

"It's just that I think this 'happy event' should take place in the privacy of your bedroom, preferably with someone you love."

Preferably with him. But if he even hinted at such a thing, she was liable to hit him with her pocketbook. Unfortunately, the subtle approach wasn't working with her. And she only laughed, thinking he was joking whenever he tried the direct approach. Which left the sneaky approach.

He'd have to give that some thought.

"That's easy for you to say. You go out. You have dates." April shifted her purse strap to the other shoulder. "Do you have any idea how scarce eligible men are in Bliss County?"

Colton moved his foot in front of the door and relaxed his grip on the handle. "Your mother says you're too picky, and I happen to agree with her."

April rolled her eyes. "Don't get me started on that."

A woman in her fifties approached them with an armful of manila folders. The punch-label name tag on her brightly flowered dress read Aunt Sophie, Office Manager.

"My, my, my! Is this any way to begin what could be the happiest event of your life?"

Colton caught the smirk April sent his way.

The woman directed her attention to April. "What is your name, dear?"

"Hanson. April Hanson."

"Yes, of course! You're right on time. Why don't you come in, and I'll have you fill out a medical history form."

They accompanied her to the desk, and April jutted her

chin and maneuvered so that the office manager walked between them. But the overly familiar woman paid no heed to the tension between them and carried on an uncensored monologue about the many fertility problems she'd seen and the clinic's high success rate for pregnancies.

"If at first you don't succeed," the woman said cheerily, "well, we'll keep trying until you do."

At the desk, she picked up a clipboard and handed it to April. "I love this job. I don't have any children of my own," Sophie confessed, "but I feel like an honorary aunt to the hundreds of babies who've come along since I started working here."

That would explain the name tag, April thought.

"In fact, two of them have been named after me."

At that, Colton added dryly, "Girls, I hope."

Aunt Sophie giggled. "You're such a kidder!" Then, to April, she added, "Good-looking, and funny, too. You're a lucky gal."

April just smiled in response and took the form to the waiting room. Although there were a couple of sofas, she chose to sit in a chair in the corner, away from the others. Maybe Colton should have let her come by herself. By being here, his only accomplishment was in making them both miserable. He took a seat on the opposite side of the room.

"Mr. Hanson," Aunt Sophie called. Colton looked up and was surprised to find her looking at him. He checked to see if there might be another man in the room, but there were only three women.

When he approached the desk, he corrected the mistake. No sense in making things worse. "I'm not Mr. Hanson," he said. "The name is Radway."

The woman pushed her glasses down on her nose and peered over them. "I see," she said, although it was clear she didn't. She handed him a clipboard, and in her characteristically loud voice, said, "We'll need you to fill this out, and soon we'll call you back to the examining room where the doctor will measure the size of your, um, you know...family jewels."

By now, April had apparently forgotten about their tense encounter of a few minutes ago. Instead, she seemed to be enjoying herself ... and his discomfort.

"After that," Aunt Sophie continued in the same loud voice and gestured down the hall, "you'll take your cup into that room where you'll watch a movie with no plot. Then, *voila,* pretty soon you and *Miss* Hanson will be in the family way."

He could have sworn he heard a snicker from April's corner of the room. "I'm afraid you're mistaken," he informed her. "I'm not the donor."

The woman's demeanor changed from disapproval to one of sympathy. She patted his hand. "Don't take it personally," she said in an attempt at a whisper. Unfortunately, her booming voice seemed to be stuck at high volume. "Lots of men have sleepy tadpoles."

By now, April was cracking up. He glared at her, and it seemed to make an impression when she took a more serious attitude and came to stand beside him. She looped her arm through his and sidled close beside him.

"It's okay, honey," April said, her voice oozing sympathy. "I love you just the way you are."

"But I..."

Colton darted a glance from one woman to the other, realizing he was going nowhere fast. It was bad enough she'd come here against his advice. It was worse that she was determined to have a strange man's baby when all she needed to do was open her eyes and look around her. But now, to top things off, his potency was suddenly the scrutiny of everyone within earshot.

"You were right, dear," he said, taking April's hand from the crook of his arm.

The women in the waiting room were openly watching the soap opera unfolding before them.

It was plain to April that her teasing was about to backfire on her. She eyed him warily as he turned slightly, his voice carrying toward their audience in the waiting room.

"I've been taking this all too personally. It doesn't matter who the genetic father is..."

He paused dramatically.

"...as long as we love each other."

April looked at him as if he'd lost his mind. She tried to pull away, but Colton held her hand tightly in his.

"This has been a difficult time for me—for *both* of us."

He lifted her hand to wipe away an imaginary tear at the corner of his eye, then held her palm against his cheek. When he kissed her fingers, April felt herself go weak in the knees.

"But you've been the strong one throughout. I love you, April." His voice cracked ever so slightly. "I always have, and I always will."

She heard a tiny sniff from the otherwise silent waiting room. Not so much as a magazine page crackled, not that three-year-old, finger-worn paper crackled anyway. Her lips were parted slightly as she started to say something in response, but she didn't know quite what.

Before she could react or even think of a funny rejoinder, Colton took advantage of her silence. He bent and touched his lips to her mouth. Once the kiss began, all thoughts fled her mind. All she could focus on was savoring the tantalizing nearness of him.

His hands were warm and firm as they slid along her sides. She tensed as his fingertips made their way to her back, where they slid down to rest just above the curve of her bottom. She trembled in his arms and knew her reaction had nothing to do with the cold blast from the air conditioner.

Her mouth softened under his kiss. Despite her initial resistance, she responded to his kiss, lifting her chin to offer full access to her lips, her neck, and...

Colton glanced downward, and April became aware of his heated gaze. Crazily, she wanted his trail of kisses to trace the path that his eyes followed.

He'd kissed her before, once in the sandbox at nursery school after she got sand in her eyes, and once during a truth-or-dare game at a birthday party. And then there was that time before either of them had experienced their first boy/girl, on-the-lips kiss. They'd been so afraid of making an embarrassing mistake on a date that they'd practiced on each other ahead of time.

Her reaction to that practice kiss had been rather pleasant, in a teenage sort of way, but it was nothing compared to what she felt now.

Colton loosened his grip on her waist. He felt a prickling of regret for his behavior. This kiss had started as a prank to get even for the public wisecrack she'd dealt. But now the joke was on him.

As much as he hated to do it, he had to end the kiss before he dragged her into that room with the plotless movie and inseminated the hell out of her.

April wanted Buddy to finish what he'd started. She wanted him to deepen the kiss and plunder her lips until the scorched flesh of her mouth melted beneath his own. Instead, he pulled away, but only slightly, granting her a view of the deepest, brownest eyes that existed in all of Bliss. His eyes were shuttered so that she had difficulty reading the emotion behind his dark lashes. Again, he kissed her—two quick pecks that teased rather than satisfied—and pulled away before she could fully realize the magnitude of what had just transpired between them.

April's knees almost buckled when he released her. Placing a hand on the reception desk to steady herself, she stared at the man who had so thoroughly turned the tables—and turned her heart upside down—after her joking remark.

Aunt Sophie cleared her throat. "Um, if you two are finished, Miss Hanson, the doctor will see you now."

3

April was still thinking about Buddy's unexpected behavior that evening at her mother's house as they discussed the upcoming family reunion.

"Are you sure you're reserving the campground just for us?" Joan Hanson asked her daughter. "It's hard enough for some of the older people to sleep in those hard beds— in those un-air-conditioned cabins, I might add—without a bunch of midnight kumbaya-ing from the youth groups you and Colton always have there."

April took a deep breath. *Count to ten,* she told herself. Before she made it to five, her mother launched into a commentary about the family members who would be coming.

"If your cousin Ardath has gotten any fatter than she was last year, you're going to have to reinforce the picnic benches. I swear, she must die of embarrassment at weddings and funerals, what with her panty hose making that god-awful swishing sound every time her thighs rub together." She passed a pencil across the kitchen table to April. "Make a note to make Ardath play softball. Heaven knows, the girl can use the exercise."

Although her mother came across like a steamroller some-times, April knew she meant well. Joan's actions— and her sometimes callous comments—were, in her own misguided way, a demonstration of love and concern for her family members.

Even so, April refused to join in on her mother's well-intended meddling. "Mom, I'm not going to make anyone—"

"And hide the beer from your uncle Joseph. The doctor told him to stay away from the stuff. Besides, we don't want him making a public spectacle of himself like he did last year. The neighbors are still talking about that wheelbarrow inci-dent." Joan patted her lap in invitation to her smash-faced Himalayan cat who wound around the leg of her chair and then snootily sauntered off. Instead, Maybelline answered the invitation and left a wet nose print on the elder Hanson's bare knee. Joan wiped her knee and continued her train of thought.

"I certainly don't want to give the gossips any new ammu-nition to hurl at your poor uncle Joseph."

April picked up the pencil and scribbled a note under the list of items to buy. Her mother leaned forward and read it, upside down.

"What do you need duct tape for?"

"To tape something shut," April said innocently. She studied her mother's mouth and decided she'd need an extra-wide roll.

"And speaking of beer and public humiliation, what's this I hear about you and Colton getting thrown in jail for selling beer without a liquor license?" Joan ran a hand through her frosted hair and gave a beleaguered sigh. "It was bad enough that your sister's reputation suffered in high school. I won't have you ruining your reputation, as well."

April pressed her fingers to her eyebrows and tried to rub away the tension as she'd seen Buddy do so many times. "Did you speak to Nicole?"

"No. Is Nicole involved, too? I read about it in the paper." She got up and retrieved the thin weekly newspaper from the sofa. After opening the *Bliss Crier* to the middle, she spread it out in front of April and pointed a finger at the picture that accompanied the short article. "This guy here—the one who looks like Elmer Fudd—says he arrested you for breaking the liquor laws."

April sighed. "It was a misunderstanding."

Joan's eyes glittered with moisture, and April had the strong sense that her mother was about to launch into manipulation mode.

"You were always such a good girl. I always bragged about you because you never gave me a moment's trouble. I was even going to give you something special ... you know, a family heirloom to signify how much you mean to me."

April was right. *Major* manipulation mode.

"But I suppose I could always give it to Nicole instead. After all, Grandma Hanson's quilt should stay in the family, and I don't hold the circumstances of Nicole's pregnancy against her."

"Are you talking about the Hanson family quilt that has a story behind each patch?"

Joan nodded.

It had started out as her great grandmother's lap robe. As events had unfolded in the course of her family members' lives, patches got added to the border until it was now large enough to cover a twin-size bed.

A child's bed.

Her child's bed.

As a young girl, April had loved pointing to the various colored squares as old seventy-eights played on the ancient

Victrola, and hearing her grandmother tell why that particular scrap of fabric had been added to the quilt. If she thought about it long enough, she could probably recall all the squares and the story that went with each. There was a square of white lace from her great grandmother's wedding dress, a blue square from her father's Cub Scout uniform, the pink teddy bear design from Stella's favorite shirt in kindergarten, and there was even a patch of canvas from the tent that blew down during one of their early family camping trips before the divorce. Stella had once called her a sentimental twit for getting so attached to the quilt, but April had never been able to explain why it was more than a mere blanket to her.

April stood and emptied her cold coffee into the sink. Deep down, she knew her mother would never defy Grandma Hanson's last wishes. But for her to even hint at such a thing clearly indicated how strongly she felt about April keeping her good name intact. The whispers that followed Stella's indiscretion had wounded Joan deeply, and April didn't want to put her through the same kind of heartache and disappointment.

The newspaper rustled as her mother refolded it. "Don't let me down." The gentleness and sincerity of Joan's plea weakened April more than even the best staged manipulation.

Still, she couldn't resist testing the waters. Self-consciously folding her arms over her abdomen, April leaned against the sink. "So, if I were to, say, go to a fertility clinic and get pregnant with a stranger's baby, you'd disown me?"

"I'd never disown you!" Joan stood and pushed her chair under the table. "But I don't like you joking about something like that. Someone might hear you and think it's true."

April felt her emotions go limp. She would never convince her mother that having a child this way was a socially accepted option these days. But there was no way April would give up her wish to have a baby.

With a little careful planning, she could have the baby she so desperately wanted and still spare her mother the disappointment of another grandchild born out of wedlock.

With a barely suppressed smile of triumph, April gathered the list and pencil she'd left lying on the table. It would take some thought, but she was determined to have her cake and eat it, too.

The hard part would be persuading Buddy to buy out her half of the campground.

In preparation for April's upcoming family reunion, Colton painstakingly vacuumed the pool while Clyde killed weeds that had sprouted through cracks in the concrete apron.

Colton was worried about April. But that was par for the course with them. He'd been looking out for April for as long as he could remember. This time, however, he didn't know how to bail her out of the problem that was eating at her.

Her biological clock was ticking, and it was obviously driving her nuts. She'd always mothered anyone and anything that would let her. When they were kids, there had been kittens, dogs, and even a baby bird that had tumbled out of its nest. Now there were Steven, Clyde, the baby squirrel, and the myriad children for whom she organized recreational activities. And heaven help him if he should come down with a cold. April went into high gear mothering mode whenever anyone got sick.

She wanted a family, and he wanted more than anything to be a part of it, agreement be damned. Colton stabbed the skimmer into the water and rescued a fat black cricket.

When she'd married Eddie Brock, his so-called best

friend, Colton felt as though a huge piece of himself had died. For some reason, he'd thought she would still be there when he got back from college. He had hoped that their time apart would affect her as deeply as it did him and that she'd realize the lifelong caring between them could, and *should,* go beyond mere friendship. As a shy, inexperienced teen, he'd been reluctant to risk rejection by suggesting a romantic relationship. Ever since, he'd regretted his hesitation.

They had kept in touch throughout her marriage, but their emails and phone conversations were polite and ever so platonic. After the divorce, rumors went around that he was the reason for her and Eddie's breakup. Colton didn't care what people said about him, but he sure as heck didn't want them making up stories about April. So, when he came back to Bliss as her business partner, he started dating women left and right, just to prove the town gossips wrong. What they didn't know was that—no matter how beautiful or alluring his dates were—he'd much rather be with April.

Some of Colton's married friends envied him his vast collection of girlfriends. What they didn't know was that he envied *them* the permanent relationship they had with the one special woman they loved.

He turned to hang the skimmer on the chain-link fence, and Clyde lifted his attention from the dandelions beside his wheelchair. The older man stared past the empty playground toward the dirt and gravel road leading to the campsites. A woman with short blonde hair jogged toward them, waving her arms and shouting something.

"Is that April?" Clyde asked.

Colton took notice of the pendulous attributes that bounced beneath the woman's T-shirt with her every step, then called up a mental image of his petite, pert business partner in a knit tank top. "No, April's smaller." After he'd said the words, he hoped Clyde would assume he was referring to her height.

"I think she's the one at site R-17," Clyde said. "She and her husband have that blue Winnebago."

Colton remembered now. "And the little girl that April went goofy over."

"That's the one."

Adjusting the brim of his Stetson, Colton stepped through the gate and jogged across the grass to see what the matter was. Behind him, the wide tires of Clyde's chair crunched on the gravel driveway.

Although the woman appeared to be only about thirty years old, the physical exertion caused her to breathe heavily, as if she were older than he guessed or maybe just out of shape. A cold trickle of dread traced a path down Colton's spine as he considered the other alternative ... fear.

By the time he reached her, she was incoherent, her voice high-pitched with panic. Colton stilled her flailing arms and forced her to look squarely at him. Using his most authoritarian demeanor, he spoke with strained calmness.

"Slow down. You'll have to tell me what's wrong if you want me to help you."

Clyde wheeled up to them. "Bee sting?"

She wiped away tears with the handkerchief Colton had given her and tried again to tell him what had happened. He was able to make out the words *my baby* and *lost*.

Clyde made a quick U-turn with his wheelchair. "You go," he urged Colton. "I'll call for help."

As Colton raced off with the mother of the missing girl, he hoped Clyde would be careful about how he phrased the situation to April. The last thing he needed was to have her add her own fears to the mother's.

April and Maybelline arrived at the campsite mere seconds after they did. The father pushed aside a leafy branch and emerged from a wooded path behind their campsite. The look he flashed his wife told Colton all he needed to know. The toddler was still missing.

Mr. Kohlman was more helpful in describing what had happened than his wife had been. As he spoke, Colton noticed that April instinctively put her arm around the younger woman's shoulders. She was taking this personally, he could tell. Her lips flattened in a tight line, and the father explained how two-year-old Kimberly had seen a rabbit just beyond their picnic table and had apparently followed it into the woods. She must have slipped away in the short time that he lit coals for a hot dog lunch and Mrs. Kohlman went inside for plates and potato chips. Colton sympathized with the distressed couple, but he had an even stronger urge to comfort April the way she sought to reassure the mother.

Instead, he started issuing orders. In their distress, the Kohlmans appeared relieved to have someone take charge for them. Colton handed Mrs. Kohlman the walkie-talkie April had given him.

"You stay here in case Kimberly comes back on her own," he said. "Mr. Kohlman, you fan out to the left. I'll take the center area, and April, you go to the right. We'll meet back here in twenty minutes."

When April hung back, he watched her pick up a yellow scrap of fabric from the picnic bench. "Is this Kimberly's?" she asked Mrs. Kohlman.

The woman nodded, clutching the walkie-talkie to her chest like a lifeline. "That's Kimmy's blankie."

At the affirmative statement, April bent and held the fabric to Maybelline's nose. Colton shook his head at the idea of that flea-brained dog tracking a child by scent. The canine might be a golden retriever, but it seemed clueless as to the meaning behind its breed name.

He couldn't stand around and let her waste precious time.

"Forget it, April. That dog doesn't even know how to fetch a newspaper."

She looked hurt, and he instantly regretted his words. But April should know by now that the dog wasn't very smart. She herself had been trying, without luck, for the past few weeks to teach it to fetch the paper.

April, however, seemed determined that her plan would work. "Go kiss the baby," she told the dog.

Colton shrugged his shoulders and trudged off into the woods. The only thing April had been able to teach the dog—who loved tiny children perhaps as much as April did—was to lick a toddler's bare knees or forearms rather than jump against him. Colton supposed the only reason the dog consented to the behavior modification was because of the delighted laughter brought on by the "kisses." If the antici-pated reward of a giggling baby inspired Maybelline to hunt down the child, more power to her. Unfortunately, Colton didn't hold much hope that the animal would be of help.

At least the weather was warm. Although there was no danger of exposure, Colton worried that the little girl might stumble into a nest of yellow jackets. Or, if her tiny legs took her far enough, the creek posed a threat. The bright sun faded as though someone had hit a dimmer switch, and the sky darkened, warning of an afternoon thunderstorm. He stepped over a fallen tree, calling the child's name as he pushed his way through the canopy of new foliage. They would have to hurry if they were to find the girl before the storm hit.

When he eventually returned to the campsite, he was disappointed to learn that no one had had any luck finding Kimberly. But he wasn't half as upset as April seemed, though he wasn't sure whether her attitude was because of not finding Kimberly or because she was now talking to her personal adversary, Alexander Dugg.

Colton stepped forward, prepared to mediate if necessary. A cluster consisting of Steven and about a dozen strangers—probably folks who'd heard about the lost child on their police scanners—gathered around the pair, listening as they debated the best plan for finding the kid.

"Afternoon, Deputy Dugg."

April watched as the deputy looked up at the towering tree of a man who stood before him with his right hand extended. Dugg stared at the huge palm and thick fingers, obviously unsure whether this former inmate—albeit a temporary one—was still angry with him. She could almost see the gears turning in the little man's brain. If he put his own squat hand in that big one, he might never practice shooting his gun again. And then any chances for becoming sheriff would be zilch.

The deputy must have decided to risk it and was overtly relieved when the squeeze was only uncomfortably tight. He flexed his fingers, glancing up at Colton to see if he was silently laughing at him. But there was no smile on the big man's face. Colton seemed more concerned about the child than about goading him. April wondered whether the deputy felt relieved or inconsequential.

"Buddy, I'm glad you're here," she told her partner. "Dugg here is trying to tell all these people to go home, but we need them to help search."

"Great. Just great," Dugg said. "You're gonna try to undermine my authority right here in front of all these civilians." The squat man took on an air that seemed to indicate he would nip that in the bud. "This is a police matter, Miss Hanson. Untrained citizens have no business interfering in criminal matters."

"Criminal matters!" April flung her arms, and the deputy dodged. "Buddy, are you going to kick him off our property, or am I?"

The deputy cleared his throat. "It's possible that this is actually a kidnapping. I'm going to have to question Mr. Kohlman."

He reached into his shirt pocket to retrieve the small notepad he kept there, but he was stopped by a powerful grip on his wrist.

"Hey!"

The fierce gaze that met his eyes brooked no argument. "Time's a'wasting," Colton said quietly. "There's a scared little girl out there waiting for us to find her. I suggest you form a line with all these other nice people and focus on finding the girl."

April was relieved when the deputy did as he was told, moving in beside Steven. But her relief didn't last long.

"I heard about your fondness for naked dolls," he told the teen. "How do we know *you* didn't have something to do with the kid's disappearance?"

The punch to the deputy's gut seemed to come out of nowhere. In the next moment, he and the lanky teen were rolling in the dirt. Although Dugg clearly had the weight advantage, Steven's surprise attack and anger overcame it. To the law enforcer's obvious embarrassment, he was quickly pinned and straddled by the young streetfighter. He raised his arms to fend off the rain of blows.

Though they both knew the deputy deserved whatever was coming to him, Colton plucked Steven off him, and April helped Dugg to his feet. Shaking her off, the deputy brushed the dirt from his uniform that, prior to this, had been crisply starched.

The flat of April's hand hit him against the side of the head, and Dugg immediately reached up to touch his throbbing temple. Although the beaning had been an automatic reaction, she recovered quickly and retrieved a bit of vegetation from his hair.

"Grass," she offered by way of explanation.

"Don't expect me to thank you," he said, still rubbing the side of his head.

"If you say so much as one word in retaliation to Steven," she warned, "I'll, I'll—" She looked at Colton to enlist his help.

"Tell the IRS he cheated on his taxes?" her partner suggested.

The little deputy clutched his chest. "You wouldn't!"

"Come on," said Colton, nudging them both toward the woods where the volunteer searchers had gone. "We have work to do."

A couple of times, April thought they had found the child, but once it had only been a pile of dry leaves and the other time the rustling behind a tree came from two gray squirrels playing tag. And with each false alarm, Deputy Dugg had started to step forward to claim the rescue as his own.

April rolled her eyes as she imagined what was probably going through his head. *Sheriffs Candidate Rescues Toddler from Certain Death.* But she doubted that even a headline like that would help his campaign. Apparently, Maybelline agreed. Each time the deputy went near April, the yellow dog bared her teeth and growled at him.

They searched for almost an hour more. By then the wind moved in menacing gusts around them, pelting them with occasional large droplets of rain as thunder rumbled a warning in the distance.

April rubbed her bare arms and turned the collar up on her shirt. They were nearing the creek that cut across the back border of the campground, but still no sign of the little girl. April's voice was hoarse from hollering Kim's name, and her bare legs and arms were covered with scratches from sticks and thorns, but she wouldn't give up. The first time she had seen the dark-haired, blue-eyed toddler, she'd fallen in love with her. She hated to think of that sweet little child alone, afraid, and crying for her mother.

Maybelline had lost interest shortly after they'd started their search, preferring to spook rabbits and quail out of their hiding spots. So much for that bright idea.

A shout sounded through the woods to the left of her. It was Colton, and he sounded excited. Heedless of the briars that snagged her ankles, April joined some of the others in running toward him.

A circle of searchers gathered around the tiny form stirring from her napping place beside a cluster of newly sprouted wildflowers. Colton knelt beside her, his voice low and calm to avoid startling her. "Hi, sweetheart. Did you have a nice nap?"

She nodded, obviously unaware of the commotion she had caused, and rubbed her eyes with a chubby fist. "I saw de Easter bunny," she declared.

"Well, let's go back to your campsite so you can tell your mama and daddy all about it." Despite the increasing rain, Colton remained kneeling and casually held out a hand to her.

April's heart swelled with pleasure. She couldn't help being proud of her friend's reassuring way with the child as he quickly and easily gained her trust.

Little Kimmy was reaching out to take his hand when Officer Dugg stepped away from the group of onlookers and snatched her up into his arms.

"We'd better get this kid out of here before lightning hits."

Kim screwed her face up and popped her bottom lip out a

split second before she bawled with a force and resonance that would have done any opera singer proud.

Colton stepped toward Dugg, then hesitated. April could see that he didn't want to get into a tug-of-war over the child. She moved to his side and prepared to give the deputy a piece of her mind for scaring the child as he had. But as she passed Dugg, the toddler leaned toward her, holding out her arms and bawling even louder.

Dugg seemed even more confused than April by the child's reaction. Rather than argue with the screaming child, he wordlessly handed her over to April.

Rain plastered the girl's dark pageboy hair to her round face as treetops danced the hula in the wet breeze. But April didn't notice any of that as Kimmy's soft arms went around her neck, and the child snuggled against her.

"It's okay, sweetheart. I won't let anything happen to you." April tucked her chin against the tiny shoulder and understood with heartbreaking clarity the deep-seated need that had been driving her to have a child of her own. All her protective urges surfaced, and she held the toddler tightly, as if afraid of losing her yet again.

Colton wrapped his shirt around Kimmy, who was now sucking her thumb, and walked with April back to the campsite. Mr. Kohlman met them halfway, having heard the shouts where he had been searching. Kimmy eagerly went to her joyous father, leaving an aching emptiness in April's chest.

As if sensing her loss, Colton wrapped an arm around her shoulders. Grateful for the comforting gesture, April leaned against her friend, drawing from his ever-present strength. Rain trickled down through the crisp curls of his brown hair, and goose bumps flecked his tanned skin.

April looked up at him as they walked, a smile curling her lips. "Are you cold or just glad to see me?"

Colton grinned down at her and squeezed her shoulder. "A little of both, I guess."

He tugged the limp brim of his hat. When rainwater funneled off onto April, he sheepishly took it off, baring his head to the steady patter.

"That was sweet the way Kimmy took to you," he said.

Pushing the soggy strings of hair away from her face, she shook her head. "I must have reminded her of her mother. We look somewhat alike, you know."

"Not really." He grinned again as if he were enjoying a secret joke.

April didn't even bother to ask. Instead, she blurted what she'd been wanting to tell him since her conversation with her own mother.

"I'm going to leave town, and I want you to buy out my half of the campground."

He drew his thumb in a circle on her shoulder. "Look, I know you're upset about the little girl getting lost, but this is the first time it's happened in the six years we've owned this place. Don't you think maybe you're overreacting?"

"It has nothing to do with Kimmy. Well, I take that back. She made me see how much I want and need a baby of my own." April stopped in her tracks and faced her partner, oblivious to the rain soaking them both. "I've held other people's babies before, but this was somehow different. Did you see the way she held out her little arms to me? And the way she snuggled against me as though she trusted me to take care of her and make everything all right?"

April wrapped her arms around her waist, savoring the sweet memory of it.

"Holding and comforting that little girl made me see so clearly what I've been missing without a child of my own. Buddy, I need to do something now."

Colton turned away from her and started walking back

toward the Kohlmans' campsite, hesitating as she fell into step beside him.

"What about the campground? This was *your* baby. You're the one who found it; you're the one who negotiated the deal, and you're the one who suggested I leave my job in Pennsylvania to become your partner. What am I supposed to do while you're away getting yourself pregnant? And more importantly, how are you going to do it without your family finding out? Your mother will certainly have something to say about it."

Colton reached up and kneaded the spot between his eyebrows.

"I'll miss the campground, but right now a baby is more important to me," April said softly. "But I know that whatever price you offer for my share of the business will be fair, and I'm willing to accept payment in monthly installments. It doesn't have to be much ... just enough to pay for an apartment and fertility treatments."

His jaw clenched, signaling his displeasure with the whole situation, but April wouldn't let his reaction stop her. This was too important to let a little disapproval stand in her way. Not even Colton's disapproval.

"As for my mother," she continued, "I'll move out of town —maybe out of state—and let her think I eloped with somebody I met there. After the artificial insemination is successful, I'll announce my pregnancy, then get a 'divorce' and move back home."

He was persistent, just as she knew he would be. "Have you considered just telling your mother what you want to do? She may surprise you and be very supportive."

She could tell even as he said the words that he didn't believe them.

"It was bad enough that Stella got pregnant by accident."

She blew out a sigh. "It would kill my mother to know that her single daughter got pregnant on purpose."

The rain was pouring now, but the sun surprised them by popping out from behind a cloud. Neither of them increased their pace. It wasn't the first time they'd been caught in a sudden shower.

Colton reached out and took her hand in his. "I don't want you to go away," he confessed. "I need you here."

April pressed his callused hand. "I'm sure you'll be able to find someone to take my place."

He shut his eyes. "Never."

The patter of the rain against the leaves abruptly ended, filling the woods with an eerie silence in the moments before the birds and crickets resumed their chirping.

"Oh, come on. Now *you're* the one who's overreacting."

He stopped, turning to face her fully, her hand still held captive in his. "What will it take to keep you here?"

"There's really no point in discussing it, because my mind is—"

"I've got it," he declared. "I have a solution that'll suit both of our needs."

"You do?"

"*I'll* give you a baby!"

✣ 4 ✣

April tried to pull her hand from his grasp, but he held tight. "Look, if this is one of your daily date requests, it's not very funny. I'm serious about this, and I need to know whether you're interested in helping me. If not, just say so, and I'll find another way to do it."

"I *am* interested in helping you ... that's what friends are for. And I'm very serious about my offer."

She was skeptical. Friends did help each other, but this seemed excessive, even for best buddies like themselves. "Having trouble getting a date for this weekend?" she teased.

Colton turned toward the office and resumed walking, letting their joined hands swing with each stride. "Could you accept my offer better if you thought I had an ulterior motive?"

She looked up at him and was suddenly, acutely aware of his bare chest. She had seen him shirtless before, but she'd always looked at him as one would a brother. Although he'd jokingly asked her for a date on a regular basis, she'd never taken him seriously. At least, she *thought* he'd been joking at the time. "It would be more believable," she admitted.

"You want a baby. I want you to stay here and continue as my partner at the campground. This way both of us will be happy."

"You always told me it's not good to mix business and pleasure."

"We'd be mixing business and business. Your business is to start a family. My business is to keep this campground running smoothly."

"You scratch my back, and I scratch yours?"

He smiled and squeezed her hand. "Among other things."

April's feet grew roots. Patiently, as always, Colton stopped to wait for her. The problem was that he now faced her, and his naked chest was right at her eye level. She tried to ignore the breadth of his shoulders and the flatness of his stomach. Even more, she tried not to imagine the intimate activity he was suggesting they engage in to produce the baby she wanted.

"You're not really serious about this."

He tucked a finger under her chin and lifted it until her gaze met his own. Even more than staring at his chest, April found it difficult looking him in the eye. "I'm as serious as you are about wanting a baby," he said.

Her breath caught in her throat. "That's pretty serious."

He nodded. There was no hint of mischief in his eyes, no quirking of his lip as when he tried to suppress a grin. He was serious.

She couldn't ask for a better donor. Physically, he was in great shape. Lean, yet muscular. She couldn't remember the last time he'd been sick.

He was smart, too. In just a few short years, he'd helped turn the campground around from the brink of bankruptcy to a thriving, growing business.

And with his expressive eyes, firm jawline, and well-defined facial features, there was no doubt he'd sire beautiful offspring.

This was crazy! She was thinking about him as if he were a stallion at stud. And, as with Daisy's moment of indiscretion, there most certainly would be a high price to pay later.

She shook her head. "The reason I'm going away to have a baby," she reminded him, "is to avoid the stigma that hung over Stella and Nicole. I want to raise my child in Bliss County, and the only way to do it in peace is to abide by tradition and get married."

"Okay," Colton said easily. "Then I'll marry you. If you decide you don't want to remain married after you conceive, we can get a friendly divorce."

April patted her friend's arm. "I've already ruined one friendship by marrying the guy, and I don't believe in making the same mistake twice. As for divorce, I never want to go through that again, especially not with a baby involved." Impulsively, she stood on tiptoe and kissed her friend's cheek. "It was very sweet of you to make such a generous offer. You're a good friend, Buddy."

That was a close call. For a moment there, she had started to seriously consider his suggestion. She supposed it would be better for both of them—and their friendship—if she put a close to the conversation.

"So, then it's a deal. You'll buy out my share of the campground; I'll leave town to get pregnant, and if all goes well, I could be back working with you within a year or two."

"Tell you what, we don't have to get married legally," Colton persisted. She wasn't sure, but it seemed as though a lightbulb had switched on over his head. Before she had time to consider its meaning, he spilled his idea. "If you're worried about your family and the town gossips, we could put on a mock marriage with a phony preacher. Then, once you get pregnant, we can split up without the hassle of a legal divorce."

His voice was too calm, too casual for the enormity of what he was suggesting. Although he watched for her reaction, he wouldn't meet her eyes. April supposed he was trying not to let on how important the success of the campground was to him. In her concern about planning for a baby, she had failed to consider the harmful impact her leaving would have on their business. On Colton's livelihood. It wouldn't be fair of her to abandon him just as the campground was starting to turn a healthy profit. On the other hand...

"It wouldn't be fair of me to *use* a friend like that," she said, dismissing the tempting thought.

He gave a cockeyed grin. "I've been used in worse ways."

Turning away from her, he picked up a large rock from the dirt path and tossed it into the woods. "I suggest you make up your mind pretty quick. Your family reunion next month would be a great time for a wedding."

The more April thought about it, the more she supposed Colton's crazy plan could work. In the past couple of days, since he'd first suggested the unorthodox arrangement, she could think of little else. She'd finally come to the conclusion that since she was going through the insemination procedure anyway, it might as well be with a donor whose background she knew. And in the meantime, the pretense of marriage to Colton would be believable and acceptable to her old-fashioned family and neighbors.

April propped an elbow against the store counter and tipped the doll bottle up so the squirrel could drain the rest of the milk formula the veterinarian had prescribed for it.

For as long as she could remember, Colton had been there

for her. Whenever she'd needed a study partner in school, he was right there. When she'd needed a partner to help her buy and manage Cozy Acres, he'd quit his job in Pennsylvania and returned to Virginia. And now that she wanted a baby, he was willing to help her once again ... his most personal offer yet.

The bell over the door jangled as Colton entered the store. Sweat glistened at his temples and dampened the hair at the back of his neck. He held out a lush bouquet of brown-eyed Susans. She accepted the proffered bundle, and he brushed a blonde tendril away from her cheek.

"When I saw these, they reminded me of your hair."

"You mean my eyes?" she asked, referring to the brown irises that used to fool strangers into thinking she was Colton's sister.

"Those, too," he agreed. His hand lingered near her face. "I was talking about the yellow petals."

It felt weird to hear him talking like this and to be on the receiving end of his undivided attention. So, to break the tension that had arisen between them, she tried to make a joke of his remark. "It must be because the petals are short and stick out all over."

Before he could continue the conversation any further, she tucked little Rocky back into his cardboard bassinet, retrieved an ice cream bar from the freezer, and handed it to the man who suddenly and inexplicably made her heart race.

He smiled his thanks, a gesture she'd seen a million times before. But today it seemed as though she were seeing it for the first time. He was a handsome man, but not overtly so. The lines of his face and body were clean and well-defined. Her friend's exterior was quite a fine package—a model of excellence for his succeeding generation—but it was his inner calm and assurance that gave his physical features their true spark. When his light-brown eyes fixed upon her, as they did now, April felt powerless to break their magnetic pull.

The phone rang on the counter, jerking her back to her senses. Grateful for the interruption, she reached for the appliance.

It was Joan. "April, I'm down at the Pantry Packer, and they have frozen hamburger patties on sale. I thought I'd get some for the reunion, but if you've already got them, I won't bother."

"Uh, now's not a good time." April really didn't want to talk to her mother right now. Not while she was still wrestling with the idea of tricking her family with a false wedding. "You see, I'm in the middle of—"

"Now is the perfect time. I'm here, and the sale ends today. Just tell me whether you want me to buy them or not."

Colton leaned against the counter. "Tell your mother I said hello."

"Is that Colton?" her mother asked.

"Yes, Mom. He said to tell you hi."

"Your cousin Earl tells me you two are getting married." Her mother sighed loudly. "I don't know why you didn't tell me about this. It's not as if I don't approve of Colton. I just wish I didn't have to hear through the grapevine about my own daughter's wedding."

April's mouth dropped open. Cousin Earl? How did he hear about it? And what other details did he—or anyone else —know about their arrangement? "Mom, we're not even sure there's going to be a wedding. All we've done is talk about it."

Joan Hanson wasted no time making plans for the event. "I suppose you'll want your father to give you away. And your aunt Freida could sing 'Oh, Promise Me.'"

"By the way," Colton piped up, "I called Earl, and he's going to be at the reunion. He said he'd be glad to perform the wedding for us."

Saluting with the ice cream bar, he threw April a

charming grin and went back outside to finish smoothing the dirt roads that led to the campsites.

Her mother's voice came through the earpiece. "At least you're not going to live in sin. You don't get any gifts when you shack up with a guy."

~

It wasn't until after Steven and Clyde had gone home for the evening that April got the chance to properly chew Colton out.

He sat on the church pew in front of the broad store-front window of the camp store, writing on the order sheet the items she called out. His right leg was propped on a pillow, and he had changed into clean shorts after showering off the dust he'd stirred up with the tractor. His outer thigh sported a white bandage where he'd been struck by a low-hanging branch after driving the tractor too close to a tree branch.

Although April had insisted that he needed antibiotic ointment for the deep scratch, he had waved away her concern, muttering something about a mother hen.

She gave a vigorous shake to a Yoo-Hoo bottle, then twisted off the cap and downed a large swallow of the choco-late drink.

He touched the bandage on his leg. "You're fretting because you're worried about me, aren't you?"

"Yeah, I'm worried I might strangle you."

He had the nerve to look surprised by her statement. "What?" he said, innocently lifting his shoulders. "What did I do?"

"Hel-looo," she said, thwacking the side of her head with the heel of her hand. "You called my cousin Earl and arranged for him to marry us."

He studied her intently. It was obvious he wasn't catching her drift. "And?"

"And I haven't even decided for sure whether I want to do it or not. Besides, Earl is a magistrate, which would make it legal. We're supposed to have a *mock* marriage, remember?"

He hesitated only a second before answering. "Ah, but that's where you're wrong. Remember when your roommate from college got married a few years ago?" Colton straightened on the bench. "And she and her fiancé wanted to have her father the preacher tie the knot on the campus grounds where they met?"

April nodded, recalling the fight her friends had over the arrangements when they learned that her father could only marry them in the town where he was licensed. "They ended up moving the wedding to her parents' backyard."

"Exactly," said Colton. "But we're not going to move the wedding, and your cousin isn't from Bliss. Hence..." he said, holding one finger aloft.

"The marriage won't be legal," April finished for him. She paced the floor in front of the cooler, having forgotten for the moment that she was supposed to be counting colas. "My aunt Freida works down at the courthouse. We could still go through the motions of buying a marriage license, but it won't be binding if the marriage isn't valid."

Colton smiled. "So, are you going to buy a new wedding dress or wear your mother's?"

She stopped her pacing and leaned against the cooler door. "What's your rush?" she asked. "Besides, you still haven't explained why Earl wouldn't know that he's not licensed to marry people outside his hometown."

"Hey, you know Earl."

She did know Earl. His forgetfulness was legendary. Her cousin took the job as magistrate to pay the bills, but his true desire was to be an artist. All his creative and mental powers went into the canvases that covered the walls of his office and home.

"All of the marriages he has performed were in his office," Colton added. "Earl said this is the first one he's had to travel to."

"I suppose that could explain why he's not up on things," April conceded. She walked past Colton and dropped the empty drink bottle into the trash can.

Colton reached out and caught her hand, letting his fingers idly graze over her bare ring finger. "Then it's settled. I'll call Earl back tomorrow and tell him it's on for sure."

Despite her initial irritation with him, April didn't resist his touch. He was a good friend—the best—for offering to do this for her. Sure, it benefited him, too, but she knew that he was equally concerned for her happiness. She squeezed his hand in return, noting the strength in it. He'd always been strong for her...protecting her and bailing her out of whatever predicament she might have gotten herself into. Once again, he was there for her. It was a lot for him to give.

And it was a lot for her to accept.

"This whole marriage setup might be make-believe, but it's still a big decision," she said at last. "I need a little more time to think it over."

It was a scorcher of a day. The humidity was so thick it seemed to suck the energy from April's body. This was not the best day for clearing tent sites of fallen debris and raking the ground smooth. But if they didn't do it today, they wouldn't get another opportunity before the tenters started arriving.

Sweat ran in rivulets between her breasts, soaking the front of her cotton shirt. Colton seemed to be no better off.

Even his hair, which usually stuck out in all directions, lay plastered to his head. Pausing in his work on the tent site beside her, he pulled his navy-blue T-shirt over his head and wiped his face with it.

The motion of April's rake slowed until finally she was leaning on the handle as she took in her partner's large shoulders, the gleaming expanse of his broad chest, and the tapering line of his waist, which seemed barely wide enough to hold up his jean shorts. A fresh bandage was taped in place above his knee, and April noticed that Colton seemed to be favoring that leg.

As if sensing her eyes upon him, he dropped the shirt to the picnic bench and looked behind him. "What?" he asked, returning his gaze to her.

Embarrassed at being caught gawking, she moved the rake in a couple of lackluster strokes. "I was just wondering what was taking Steven so long to return with the wagon," she hedged. "He should have been back by now."

Quite a while had passed since the boy had driven the tractor to a remote corner of the property where he was to unload the collected scrub for a bonfire later.

Colton picked up the saw he'd been using to cut low branches from trees. "I wouldn't worry about him. He's probably taking a break at the camp store so he can cool off in the air conditioning."

She nodded, hoping that was the case. "If he doesn't come back soon, I'm going looking for him."

Her partner grinned, pointing the saw in her direction. "Yep, you're going to make a good mama. A little overprotective, maybe, but a good one."

Steven shoved the last of the brush from the wagon onto the

pile at the back edge of the campground. Later in the evening, after the wind died down for the day, Colton would set fire to it. The thicker branches would be saved for firewood to sell to campers.

He turned the tractor back toward the tent sites where he'd left his employers, and the wagon bumped noisily behind him. At least the tent sites would be shaded, and he'd get some relief from the sun's direct rays. Steven pulled a red handkerchief from his back pocket. He wiped the cloth over his damp forehead, the action prompting the sting of a fresh sunburn.

There was a place that would be even cooler than the shaded campsites. A quick dip in the refreshing waters of the creek would be just the ticket. He was due a short break, so it wasn't like he'd be goofing off. Steven debated whether to take the brief detour. The only drawback was that, in order to get to the spot he had in mind, he'd have to cross the back corner of Killer Bea's property.

The internal debate lasted for a grand total of about three seconds. The old biddy wouldn't be out on a hot day like this, he reasoned before hanging a right at the picnic shelters. He would just have to make sure he didn't call attention to himself.

Steven killed the tractor engine out of sight of the widow's house. She was probably inside taking a nap or making those stupid dolls while listening to some old fogey music, but he didn't want to take any chances of alerting her to his plan.

Crossing the rise, he pushed aside the undergrowth that bordered the edge of the campground. April once told him that the previous owner had bought so many losing lottery tickets that he was forced to sell off this tiny corner so he could pay his property taxes.

His shirt in hand, Steven tugged the fastener on his shorts

and continued walking toward the clearing that was Mrs. Turner's yard. He climbed the fence and paused, prepared to make a quick dash down the steep slope and disappear again into the wooded area on the far side. The deepest—and coldest—part of the creek lay almost hidden amid the shaded overhang of leafy branches and vines.

He was about halfway down the sloped yard when a pink-clad figure rose up from behind the birdbath below him.

"Mrs. Turner!" Startled, Steven lost his grip on the waistband of his shorts and the unzipped fabric slipped to his ankles. Unfortunately, the momentum of his upper body continued at a rate faster than his feet. In the next instant, he was rolling downhill in a tangled mess of legs, elbows, hands, and knees. The cheap plastic birdbath did little to slow his descent, but arced upward with the impact, spilling water over the front of him as he came to a stop at the elderly woman's gray orthopedic shoes.

"Oh, dear Jesus!" Mrs. Turner picked up the empty birdbath and held it between them like a shield.

Steven leaped to his feet, the shorts still firmly anchored around his ankles. He stooped, hoping she wouldn't crown him with the lawn decoration while he reached to pull up his shorts and thus regain a shred of his dignity. The front of his skivvies was soaked.

This did not look good.

"Mrs. Turner, I can explain."

He moved closer, trying to talk to her and prevent her from blowing things all out of proportion. She took a step back and jabbed the birdbath at him.

"Rape!" she hollered, even though no one would hear her. "I'm getting raped!"

Horrified by the accusation, Steven stood dumbfounded in front of her. In that gauzy pink dress, the white-haired woman looked like a hank of cotton candy, but nowhere near as appetizing. Her lips, pursed in alarm, were the same shade of pink. And loose skin hung from under her chin and arms. He gave a grimace.

Finally, he managed to gain control of his voice. "Excuse me for saying so, ma'am, but no, thank you."

5

"I was just about to do Beachbody," Stella announced as April came into the house. "I'm streaming it on my computer. Want to join me? I'll fix us a chef salad for dinner afterward."

"Honestly, Stella, I didn't think he was your type," April teased. She ducked when her sister threw a pair of yoga pants at her.

"You can wear that. I'll get my spare."

Stella left, and April ducked into the guest bathroom to change into the stretchy black garment. Stella came into the den a moment later wearing a leopard-spotted outfit that could have come from the wardrobe of *Cats*. With her petite figure, dark-blonde hair, and large green eyes, she did indeed look like a sultry feline.

"Perfect for a grandmother-to-be," April observed.

"You're just jealous."

April lay on the floor next to her older sister and lifted first one leg and then the other. "In a way, I am," she confessed.

Stella stopped singing the "positivity" song and looked directly at her. "Of this tacky thing?"

April switched to her stomach and arched the upper half of her body off the floor. "No, of you becoming a grandmother."

"You've been spending too much time in the sun."

"It's just that you can't be a grandmother without having first been a mother."

"Wait, don't tell me," said Stella as she rose and started doing leg kicks while balancing against the back of a chair. "Your biological clock is ticking."

"Like Big Ben, it's so loud."

"So, have a baby."

She hesitated, wondering how much to tell her big sister. An unbiased opinion was what she needed, and Stella had always been honest with her. April decided on the direct approach. "I've been to a fertility clinic."

Stella ceased her leg kicks and loosened her grip on the chair back. "You still have a few more fertile years left, Baby Sis. Just give it time. You'll find someone."

Ignoring the temptation to argue with her sister about how she wanted a baby *now*, April pressed forward. "I already have a suitable donor picked out."

The two of them went back to doing leg exercises, their movements smooth and synchronized.

"If you ask me," Stella said after a moment's silence, "I think you should keep in mind that nature intended this baby making stuff to happen between a woman and a man. Not a woman and a turkey baster."

"It's not like that," April insisted. "The clinic has brought happiness to a lot of women, and the process is very professional."

"So why are you telling me all this? It sounds like you already have your mind made up."

"I've received a proposal—"

Stella's eyes gleamed with excitement.

"Only it's not the kind you're thinking of." Then she proceeded to tell her about Colton's proposal and the mock marriage he had suggested after she insisted the real thing would only ruin their friendship. "That way, he gets to keep the campground running smoothly, and I get to have a baby by way of artificial insemination and keep my reputation squeaky clean."

Switching off the computer player, Stella sat cross-legged on the floor and patted the carpet in front of her for April to join her.

"Why don't you just marry him for real? He's not Eddie Brock, you know. Besides, Colton has been in love with you for years."

"Says who?"

"Says anyone with two eyes and two ears."

"If you're talking about him asking me for dates all the time, that's just his way of joking."

Stella leaned forward and placed her hand on April's. "That's just his way of telling you he cares about you. So, when's the so-called wedding?"

"If we actually go through with it, I suppose the reunion would be a good time and place."

"May as well. It'll save you a ton of money on refreshments."

"Do you think it's a stupid idea?" April asked. "This mock marriage, I mean."

Leaning back against the sofa, Stella hugged a large green pillow to the front of her. The gesture reminded April of the times she'd had cramps and sought to ease the pain by pressing something warm and soft against her abdomen. But she knew Stella's pain went deeper than that. Her pain went to the heart.

"Nicole is the best thing that ever happened to me," she said quietly. "She means everything to me, and I want you to have someone every bit as special in your life." She gazed past April, lost for a moment in her own thoughts, before continuing. "But as much as I love her, if I had a chance to do it all over again, I'd rather not bring her into the world at all than put her through the difficult times she had to endure."

April was taken aback by her sister's honesty. "You really mean that, don't you?" At Stella's affirmative nod, she said, "Mom always claimed that she never held her granddaughter's birth against her, but I know Nicole felt responsible for the tension between you two."

"It wasn't just Mom. Besides, she meant well. It was mostly the small-minded people with their *tsk-tsk* attitudes and Nicole's classmates who wanted to know why she didn't have a daddy. That's what got to her."

April remembered the fuss that ensued after Stella had refused to name Nicole's father on the birth certificate. When Stella's young boyfriend had denied paternity, she'd insisted she'd rather her daughter have no father at all than to be rejected by the real one.

"Of course, people have become more accepting than they were twenty years ago," April suggested. "Haven't they?"

"Baby Sis, this is Bliss County you're talking about." She tossed the pillow to April. "I suggest you marry that good-looking Colton Radway and start doing the natural with him."

April moved across the bed and sized up the situation. It was scary for both of them because she'd never let him go this far before. All this time she'd been able to keep him in his place, and he'd stayed there without argument. But now, all of a sudden, he had decided he was no longer willing to stay in her pocket.

She should have seen it coming ... should have known that things couldn't remain the same forever. They had to grow or die, and now he was much more than she could comfortably handle. Their relationship had changed completely, and April was no longer the one in control. She resigned herself to letting nature take its course.

"Please come now," she begged, reaching a hand out to stroke his fur-covered body. He trembled, and she knew that even though he was the one who'd set things topsy-turvy, he was also a little afraid of taking that first step to her.

And topsy-turvy they were. In his frenzied dash into the bedroom, he'd overturned the lamp on her night table, knocked the jewelry box off her dresser, and almost pulled the curtains down on top of them.

He gazed down at her now, his eyes wide with excitement.

"Now!" April insisted more vehemently this time, but it was plain to see he was in his own little world and wasn't quite ready to satisfy her command. "Fine," she told him at last. "If you won't come to me, then I'm coming to you."

With that, she shifted her position, trying in vain to get closer to him. No luck.

"Look, I'll stand on the headboard if I have to."

Finally, in frustration, she gave up. Sprawling back on the bed, she covered her eyes with one hand.

"You males are more trouble than you're worth," she said more to herself than to the squirrel who peered down at her from atop the curtain rod.

For a moment she indulged herself in a fantasy of a world without men. Women would no longer endure wars, salary inequities, or television channels zapping by at the speed of light. Of course, there would also be no babies, no boy-cut jeans, and no one to stomp the big icky spiders that are too large for a woman's shoe to cover.

And no Colton. Suddenly this little fantasy didn't seem like much fun anymore.

The bedroom door opened, and Colton stepped inside. "I brought the pet carrier you asked for," he said, holding the tiny crate aloft.

"I thought you'd never get here," she said.

With a clarity that made her uncomfortable in its truth, she realized her relief at Colton's arrival had less to do with the squirrel's current dilemma than with her own personal feelings. Rather than examine that insight any further, she turned her attention back to the reason she'd called her friend.

"Rocky jumped out of my pocket and went tearing like a maniac through the apartment. I think he broke my potpourri jar."

"Where is he now?"

"Up there." She pointed to the top of the curtain rod where the tiny gray animal sat unsteadily, twitching his tail. "I've tried to get him to come down, but he just stares at me with those little black eyes of his."

Colton set the carrier on the floor and slipped his arm around April's waist as he helped her down off the bed. "Looks like your 'baby' is claiming his independence," he said with a chuckle.

"Well, I hope he has the good balance to go with that independence. I'm afraid he might lose his footing and fall."

This time Colton stepped up on the bed. With his long arms, he easily nabbed the squirrel and deposited it in the carrier. "You can't keep him locked up forever."

Maybelline sauntered into the room and stopped at the crate to sniff the creature inside.

April nodded reluctantly in response to her friend's

comment. This happened every time she mothered a young animal. She knew the time was coming when she'd have to turn him loose, but it always seemed to come too quickly.

"And speaking of being locked up," Colton continued as they went back to the living room, "your favorite deputy stopped by to tell me Steven is serving room detention because of what happened at Mrs. Turner's. He won't be back to work for a week."

"Poor Steven." April dropped a wedge of apple into the pet carrier and then plopped herself onto the couch. When Colton took the seat beside her, she moved her bare feet to make room for him. "The poor kid somehow manages to get himself in the wrong place at the wrong time."

Her partner nodded his agreement. When they'd decided to give the boy a part-time job and a chance to learn the satisfaction of working hard and doing a job well, they first asked about the circumstances of his incarceration. Steven's biggest crimes had been poor judgment and the lack of stability at home. He'd started running with rough friends. When one of them announced that he'd bought a used car, Steven had foolishly believed him and gone cruising with some of their friends. And when they were stopped by police, several plastic bags of illegal drugs were discovered on the back floorboard. Although Steven insisted he knew nothing about the drugs, he was unable to prove his innocence.

Once again, he was the victim of his own poor judgment. There was nothing she or Colton could do to help him out of this jam. Nothing except wait out the week and hope the experience didn't leave the boy with a desire to lash out in anger.

"What makes it worse," she added, "is that we really need him to help prepare for the reunion. He had even made a list of the chores he would do between now and then."

Colton rubbed the day's growth of stubble on his chin.

"On that list, did he happen to mention ordering a wedding cake?"

April looked down at her lap and idly rubbed the brown spot on the back of her hand. "I've been giving your suggestion some thought."

He grinned and sat up straighter. "So, you've decided to marry me?"

"*Mock* marry you," she reminded him.

"Whatever."

"I think we need to discuss the conditions before we jump into anything."

"You want to sign a prenuptial agreement?"

"Not exactly. But I do think we should discuss the arrangements first." She paused. "Just so there are no surprises for either of us."

He studied her for a moment before responding. His pale-brown eyes seemed to search her soul. "Name your terms."

April pulled her feet up onto the couch and hugged her knees to her chest. It was kind of him to do this for her, and she didn't want to insult him by laying down rules. On the other hand, she wanted to prevent any misunderstandings that could arise later.

"If your offer still stands, I'd like you to be my child's donor father." Then, lest he have any misunderstanding about that, she quickly added, "But I think we should keep that aspect of our pretend marriage purely businesslike. Which means conception will take place at the clinic."

She wasn't sure, but she thought she saw a flicker of disappointment cross his face.

Colton nodded. "Anything else?"

"Once I get pregnant, we'll get a so-called divorce before the baby is born."

"And have your family think I'm a creep for leaving you

and my unborn baby in the lurch at a time like that? I don't think so."

She laid a hand on his arm. "It'll be easier on the baby if the transition takes place beforehand rather than after."

He didn't say anything, but she could tell from the way the muscle flexed in his jaw that he didn't like this particular term. She had a feeling he wouldn't like the next one any better. But it was better to get the air cleared about it now.

"And I want sole custody of the child."

That muscle in his jaw clenched again. "I'm not going to abandon my own kid."

Regardless of whether the child was biologically his or not, and despite the fact that this was only a pretend marriage, Colton was not the kind of man who would take his duties as a father lightly. It suddenly occurred to April that his offer to shield her reputation with a mock marriage was more than a temporary acting role. It was a gift that would last the rest of his life. Her baby's birth certificate would not have a blank space where the father's name should be. Nor, she was certain, would there be a blank space in the child's life where a father should be. She knew without a doubt that he would be there for father-son camping trips or father-daughter dances, as well as birthdays, holidays, and many days in between.

"I'm sure we could work out a satisfactory visitation arrangement," she hastened to assure him.

"Then it's a deal ... you'll marry me?"

She could see the tension leave his face as she nodded her assent. Offering her outstretched hand to the man who'd been her best friend for as long as she could remember, April smiled. "It's a deal."

Colton took her hand in his, but he didn't shake on the pact as she had expected. Rising from the sofa, he pulled her to her feet to stand in front of him. "This is the kind of deal that's supposed to be sealed with a kiss."

April hesitated. "Look, I don't think—"

"I know it's awkward for you," he conceded, "but you'll have to get used to it if we're to convince your family that we're really husband and wife."

She supposed he was right, but it did seem as though things were becoming more complicated than she'd originally anticipated. Tilting her chin up, she resolutely closed her eyes and pursed her lips in a prim pucker.

His big hands went around her wrists where they dangled by her sides. April opened her eyes to see her friend smiling down at her as he placed her arms around his neck. Then his arms went around the small of her back, effectively trapping her in his embrace.

"Buddy, I—"

"Don't think of me as your buddy," he insisted. "Picture me as your husband."

There was something about the way he spoke the words, something so earnest and sincere, that the depth of it frightened April. She was still reeling from the intensity of his statement when he touched his lips to hers.

It was a warm kiss, tender and full of promises. Promises that April wasn't sure she was ready to accept. But, despite her reluctance, she found herself succumbing to the expert exploration of his mouth on hers.

She had to stand on tiptoe to avoid breaking the loop of her arms around his neck. In doing so, that brought their bodies closer, and she became aware of the heat where her torso touched his chest. A shiver of anticipation swept down her spine.

Apparently, their closeness was affecting him in a similar manner. His desire for her was evident, and it occurred to April that they were playing with fire. Her brain told her to step away from the man who was threatening to turn her life upside down, but the rest of her wanted to stay right here in the comforting circle of his arms.

She'd been behind closed office doors with Colton before, but until now she'd never imagined being behind a closed bedroom door with him. Well, maybe she had imagined it once or twice—or even three or four times – during their long friendship. But she'd never imagined herself following through on that particular daydream.

And she wouldn't, she reminded herself firmly. This marriage was to be in name only, and she would proceed with the artificial insemination, just the same as if Colton weren't the donor.

Breaking the heated contact of their lips, April looked up into the eyes of the man who'd always been her best friend and protector. He gazed back at her, his eyes full of patience and something else. Something that she wasn't sure she wanted to identify ... not just yet. For the first time since they'd known each other, she imagined Colton Radway as her husband. And the picture she saw was pleasing, in a frightening sort of way.

She hoped she was doing the right thing by pretending to marry him. More than that, she hoped they'd be able to distinguish between their pretend lives and the real ones.

"How could you let them do this?" April whispered to Colton who sat beaming beside her. "It feels like we're committing fraud."

He balanced a plateful of cake, peanuts, and butter mints on his lap. "We are," he admitted. "But we may as well enjoy it while we can. Besides, I think I heard your sister say she got a remote control caddy for me."

"We're not keeping any of this stuff. Everything stays in the box, and we're giving it all back in a few months when this charade is over."

"Spoilsport."

"Well, look at the lovebirds sitting over here whispering sweet nothings to each other," Cousin Ardath said. Then she turned toward Colton and added, "It isn't traditional to see the groom-to-be at a bridal shower."

Some men might have taken the comment as a hint that he didn't belong there, but April had long ago learned that Colton was not a typical male. He practically preened under the attention of all these women.

"April couldn't keep me away."

"Oh, what a sweet thing to say."

"No, really," April insisted. "I couldn't keep him away." She'd tried to discourage him from coming, but he wouldn't hear of it. In fact, she believed he may have even hinted to Nicole that she throw the shower. Because of that, turnabout required that April host a baby shower for her niece in a few months. She hoped that she herself would be pregnant by then.

"You two are something else," Ardath said with a giggle. Then she swished past them to get another piece of cake.

It wasn't long before the shower games started, and, of course, Colton insisted on being in the middle of them. He surprised them all by winning the prize for listing the largest number of romantic song titles, and he entertained April's relatives and friends by telling them funny stories about things April had done as a child.

And then the innuendos began. It started with a party game that required Colton to kiss her whenever she said anything relating to the bedroom. April had tried to put a stop to that, but he had insisted that she go along for fun. She gave him a glare that let him know he was wrecking what was already a sham of a bridal shower.

Once she started opening presents, the kisses increased. The set of tatted lace doilies Grandma Cole had given her for the nightstands brought a chaste peck on the lips and some amused grins from the guests. April blushed, the masquerade making her feel more and more foolish as she set about opening the next gift.

"Oops, she broke a ribbon," announced Nicole. "That means she'll have at least one baby."

April dropped the package. It seemed as though her niece had found her out, her secret exposed.

"It's a pink ribbon," Colton said with a smug smile. "Maybe that means it'll be a girl." He picked up the box and finished unwrapping it. It was an organizer rack for remote controls, and there was a pocket for holding the TV listing. He flashed a high-wattage grin at Stella and held the caddy up in a sort of salute.

Her sister shrugged. "I don't know what good it'll do you since the TV in April's living room only picks up two channels."

"That's okay," April piped up, innocently forgetting the game they'd been playing. "I have another TV in the bedroom."

At that, Stella rang a bell, and the room broke into rousing commands to "kiss the bride."

Only this time Colton's kiss was less perfunctory. April tried not to notice how soft yet firm his lips were against her own. Tried to focus on playing the act of blushing bride until the shower was over.

But Colton had another idea. Once his mouth touched hers, he was in no hurry to quit. When April tried to pull away, he slid his hand behind her neck and urged her to stay and linger a moment with him.

He was determined to win her over. With persistence and a bit of luck, she would get used to the idea of pretending he was her husband. Then it was only a matter of time before she would open her eyes to the possibility of a real marriage, complete with all the bells and whistles.

"Go, Colton," said Ardath.

By now, he could see there was no acting involved in playing her role as blushing bride. A bright-pink stain crept up her face. Apparently aware of the eyes upon them, she self-consciously averted her face. "We're embarrassing Grandma Cole," she whispered.

He glanced over at the elderly woman and gave her a good-natured wink. Her charcoal-and-snow hair in a tidy bun, Grandma Cole sat in the recliner, smiling and nodding at them. Unfortunately, it wasn't clear whether she was nodding her approval or having a spell of the palsy.

Colton handed April the next package. He had to be careful not to move too fast. It wouldn't do to let a moment of haste and carelessness undo his carefully laid plans. "Here, break another ribbon," he said, turning her attention back to the motivating force behind their make-believe union. "This one's blue."

The ribbon would have slid off without trouble, but Colton was thinking that two children—one of each sex—would be perfect. He guided her finger under the colorful strip and snapped it loose.

It was a pair of ornate silver candlesticks. Delicate silver vines wound their way up the sides, their leaves forming the well where the candle sat.

"Oh, Ardath, they're beautiful," said April. It was such a shame she'd never get the chance to use them.

Her cousin smiled shyly. "When I saw them, I thought they seemed perfect for a romantic candlelight dinner. I hope you both enjoy them."

"We will," Colton promised enthusiastically.

April glanced at Colton. He seemed to be enjoying this role he was playing. She considered suggesting he tone it down some, but there was no opportunity for her to say anything out of earshot of the others.

He turned his charm to her relatives. "Anybody got anything that'll make her say bedroom words again?" Then he winked and made fish lips at April.

Nicole passed them three large boxes in increasing sizes. "Here you go. Grandma and Mom and I chipped in together to get these for you."

They opened the middle-size box first and pulled out a tapestry garment bag. "A set of luggage," April declared.

"Hey, no fair guessing what's in the other boxes," her sister said with a hint of mischief.

Colton picked up the bag and admired it. "This'll come in handy when we go to the RV rally next winter."

"Look inside," Nicole suggested. "But be careful with the zipper."

He undid the fastener, taking care not to snag whatever was inside, and pulled out a wispy white length of fabric. Holding the thin spaghetti straps to his shoulders, Colton rose to his feet and displayed the negligee for all to see. "I think it's a bit too small."

Grandma Cole cackled at the sight, and Joan Hanson wore a sly smile as she said, "It's not for you to put *on*, Colton. It's for you to take *off*."

"Mom!" April couldn't believe her ears. She stood in indignation amid the piles of wrapping paper. After all these years of being lectured about what was and wasn't proper behavior for a lady to engage in, her mother was now making sexual innuendos. In mixed company, no less.

"It's okay, dear. This is your future husband."

"But we're not..."

"Not what, honey?" Colton prompted. He slid one arm familiarly around her waist.

He knew what she'd started to say ... that they weren't going to need the negligee because they weren't going to be making love. The clinic would be handling that aspect of their union. But that would be a foolish admission at their own bridal shower. With only a moment's hesitation, not enough to alert anyone to their shared secret, she backtracked.

"We're not going to conduct bedroom talk in public," she said primly.

Stella's bell tinkled once again, and this time Colton dipped April in Rhett Butler fashion. She clung to his neck, making the ladies in Nicole's living room think that she was enjoying it as much as they were.

To be honest, April did enjoy the thrill of having him so near, having him look at her with that steady, unflinching gaze that let a woman know she was the only one on his mind. What a wonderful actor he was.

He lowered his head to hers, and April remembered that she was supposed to breathe. Her lungs filled with air, and she was aware of her body grazing his chest. Why hadn't she ever noticed before the hardness of his chest muscles or the breadth of his shoulders?

She shouldn't let him carry this charade so far. She shouldn't let him tease her, making her want what wasn't hers to take. Most of all, she shouldn't look at him and see a man where before she had seen a dear and trusted friend. A platonic friend.

His kiss obliterated all rational thought from her mind. His arms were wrapped tightly around her, presumably to prevent her from falling, but April didn't care. She liked the feel of his body against hers, liked the way he pulled at her lips as he tenderly kissed them. Without realizing she was doing so, she was soon returning his kisses with a fervor she'd never experienced before.

"I think you should give them another present to unwrap," said Grandma Cole, "before they unwrap each other."

6

April smiled in pleasure at the blanket nestled in the second piece of luggage. "Grandma Hanson's quilt."

She unfolded it and examined the patches she had committed to memory. There was the square of white from Nicole's baptism dress, the rosebud fabric from April's prom dress, and the satin scrap saved from making Grandma Hanson's wedding dress.

It was all there, just as she remembered. She looked forward to the day she would relate the stories behind the patches to her own child.

"Thank you, Mom." She hugged her mother, hoping she would understand how much this meant to her.

"It's been a lot of years since the last patch was added," Joan said. "You'll have to start adding some of your own special memory squares."

"Yeah," Nicole teased, "maybe that negligee will have a place on there someday."

"If there's anything left of it." Stella nudged her and said in a low voice that only she could hear, "You did a pretty convincing job of making your 'engagement' look real."

April didn't look at her sister. She wasn't sure whether Stella had caught on that her response to Colton's kisses was genuine, but if she looked at her, April was sure that she would be able to read the truth in her eyes.

Colton leaned forward and pointed to a square near the edge, which indicated it was one of the pieces added later. "That reminds me of my high school football jersey."

"It is," Colton's mother said from the refreshment table. "Joan added it after you got creamed in that big playoff and broke your arm. The shirt was so mutilated that I was going to throw it away, so she just snipped out the one area that wasn't torn."

"But he wasn't a member of the family," Ardath said thoughtlessly.

Joan stiffened her posture. "Anyone who ate as many meals at my house as he did certainly qualifies as family."

April ran her fingers over the last square added. The burgundy-and-gold Cozy Acres T-shirt that she and Colton had designed and sold to campers was here on the corner. But nowhere was there a square to indicate Eddie Brock's long-ago presence in their lives. He had been her husband, but according to the family quilt, he'd never existed. However, the quilt certainly acknowledged Colton as a family member, long before they'd ever thought up this marriage farce.

Colton broke into her thoughts as he patted her hand. "This will look nice in our new apartment."

April sat bolt upright in the wooden rocking chair. "What new apartment?"

"You know," he prompted, "you've been saying you wanted a bigger place."

She didn't recall saying anything of the sort, and she didn't know why he was bringing this up now. "But I thought—"

"We don't have to move right away. But you did say you wanted an extra bedroom."

April swallowed hard. Was he bringing up their sleeping arrangements in front of her entire family? She frowned, trying to warn him with her eyes not to say anything that would lead them to suspect something was amiss with their supposed marriage.

"You know," he continued as if they'd already had a long discussion about this, "for the baby." Then to the rest of the people in Nicole's living room, he added, "We want to start trying right away."

Grandma Cole pointed her toes in delight and pressed her hands together. "Oh, how lovely."

"Then you'll want to open the next gift," Stella urged, her eyes bright with devilment. "That—and the negligee—ought to help you get a jump start on your family."

"Great." Colton ripped the paper off with glee. He pulled out a makeup case covered in a tapestry design that matched the other two pieces of luggage. "This must be for you."

April held the case on top of her lap, half afraid to open it. But the longer she waited, the more suspense she built among the onlookers in the room. Not wanting to call any more attention than necessary to this final gift, she casually popped the latch on the case and pulled out an envelope containing a hand-lettered coupon.

"It's a gift certificate," Nicole interjected, "for a three-day stay at Virginia Beach."

"But I—" April darted a glance at Colton. He looked like a kid who'd just found a bicycle under his Christmas tree. "We can't—"

"We knew you'd say that," her mother reminded her, "but it's early enough in the season for you to take a few days for your honeymoon. Whatever Clyde and Steven and your other part-timers can't handle at Cozy Acres, we'll pitch in and do."

"I'll help, too," said Verna Radway, holding her punch cup aloft. "Anything for my son and his beautiful new wife."

The envelope was becoming dog-eared under April's nervous fingers. Colton took the paper from her and set it on the floor between them. Her hands now stilled between his big palms, he lowered his voice. Concern showed in his brown eyes. "Is something wrong?"

Maybelline, who'd been napping near her feet, apparently decided now would be a good time to play catch-the-dog. The golden retriever snapped up the paper in her mouth and dashed through the living room with a half dozen women in pursuit.

Oblivious to the commotion taking place around them, April nodded in answer to her friend's question. "I forgot all about the honeymoon."

April stood waiting for her turn at bat. Mother Nature had decided to throw another scorcher at them on the day of the family reunion. She lifted the hem of her shirt and wiped her face with it.

Colton had made it to second base where he goaded Steven by lifting his foot and promptly leaping back to the safety of the padded bag a mere second before the second baseman could tag him out. After Uncle Joseph demanded the ball so he could pitch the rest of the game, Steven tossed it to him. Colton responded by taking off his shirt, snapping it at the boy, and dancing around the plate.

Standing along the fence with the rest of the lineup, April watched in amusement as their young charge took a playful swing at him. If this continued, as their horsing around often did, they'd wind up wrestling on the ground instead of playing softball.

She never tired of watching them. *Her boys*, she'd often called them. Now, she found herself focusing on the way the midafternoon sunlight caressed the firm lines of her future husband's naked back and shoulders. Shadows fell across the concave of his abdomen.

April became vaguely aware of someone standing nearby on the other side of the fence, but she was too entranced watching Colton's mad sprint to third base to see who it might be. His limbs moved like the powerful driver rods of a steam locomotive, and it was clear he was determined to let no one stop him. He was a sight to behold.

"Oh, my," came a soft whisper behind her.

Dragging her eyes away from the awesome spectacle after he made it safely home, April turned toward the sound. Mrs. Turner leaned against the fence, her lower jaw hanging slack and her hands clutching the rail.

April smiled. It wasn't the first time she'd seen a woman staring at her partner, but this broke into another age bracket. "Pretty fine sight, huh?"

Mrs. Turner met her gaze and offered up a sheepish smile. "He reminds me of my departed husband. When he was younger, of course."

"His horsing around?"

The older woman looked down at the rail she'd been gripping. "That, too."

Suddenly aware that the sun's scorching rays might be too much for the septuagenarian, April asked, "Would you like to sit down in the shade? We have refreshments."

Mrs. Turner nodded and followed her to the picnic shelter.

Once they were seated at a picnic bench and they'd had a chance to sip their fruit drinks, April couldn't help wondering what had brought their persnickety neighbor over here this time. It didn't take long to find out.

"I hate to complain," she began, and April knew that was a stretch from the truth. "But all the noise and commotion from the campground is upsetting my titmice. They haven't come to the feeder for the past couple of hours."

"It's the middle of a blistering hot afternoon," April suggested gently. "I'm sure your birds are just staying in the shade for now."

"It's not only that," she persisted. "From my screened porch, I can hear the laughter and shouting. It's enough to give a person a headache."

The open field where they were playing ball was one of the areas closest to Mrs. Turner's property, but the noise shouldn't have been loud enough to disturb her. The distance and the grove of trees between them were certain to have muted the sounds significantly.

April held her tongue for a moment, afraid that she'd say something she shouldn't. She turned her attention to the children running a relay race under the direction of Mrs. Radway and Clyde. At first, she was surprised to see such an ethnic mix among the children at her family reunion, and then she remembered that their relatives had invited friends to come with them. Their reunions had always been a more-is-merrier type of event, and April was glad her kinfolk wanted to share the fun with their friends. Clyde had often reminded her it also made business sense to expose as many people as possible to the pleasures of their campground. Potential customers, he'd called them.

"Mrs. Turner, you knew when you bought your land from Mr. Irwin that it was part of a family campground. Surely you knew that children would be laughing and playing nearby."

The older woman sniffed. "We were expecting residential neighbors. My late husband and I were of the impression that the former owner of this land would sell it off piece by piece."

"But Buddy and I bought it instead, and it remained a campground," April finished for her.

Mrs. Turner drained the last of the red drink from her paper cup. "Only busier and noisier than ever before."

She was right about that. Mr. Irwin had spent more energy and money trying to buy the winning lottery number than he'd ever put into the campground. Selling the corner of the property that now belonged to their difficult neighbor had been one of his feeble attempts to fix his financial problems, but the gambling habit had been too deeply ingrained in him. By the time April had approached him about buying the campground, he jumped at the first price she offered.

"The campground is successful," she admitted. "And we want it to continue growing."

April got up and refilled her neighbor's cup. This was the first time they'd been able to talk reasonably and rationally, and she hoped the experience would help mellow Mrs. Turner's attitude. Unfortunately, that wasn't to be the case today.

"I see that boy is back working for you."

Her words seemed like an accusation, and April immediately felt defensive on Steven's behalf. "If you're referring to the mistake he made of trespassing on your property to go swimming, then you should know he's been punished for his error in judgment."

"Mistake?" Mrs. Turner made a scornful noise. "Error in judgment? That's the problem with kids these days. People are always making excuses for them."

"And sometimes the kids who are trying to mend their ways are not allowed to live down their pasts."

They were interrupted just then by April's sixteen-year-old second cousin. The girl lifted a furry animal with a harness and leash out of the oversized pocket on her shirt. "Rocky's thirsty. Can I give him some punch?"

April trusted Jasmine to be gentle with the creature, but sometimes her Down syndrome meant she needed a little extra guidance.

"No, Jasmine, I'm sure he'd prefer water." April filled a paper cup and let Jasmine hold it while Rocky drank from it.

Mrs. Turner wrinkled her nose at the sight and turned her attention to a badly frayed woven basket on the picnic table. With a few nimble moves and some thread from her purse, she deftly finished it off and set it back on the table.

"Hey, that's cool," Jasmine said after Rocky had drunk his fill and proceeded to climb up her shirt to her shoulder. The teen stepped closer to Mrs. Turner and inspected what she'd done with the basket. "Will you show me how to do that?"

The elderly woman gave the girl a disbelieving look.

April tried to distract her cousin. No need annoying Mrs. Turner any further. "Let's check to make sure his harness and leash are secure. He's still a bit young to be out on his own."

Once she'd sent the girl on her way, she turned back to Mrs. Turner, prepared to argue further about Steven's innocence. But her neighbor was preoccupied with the goings-on at the relay race.

A little boy had been standing near the activities, leaning on crutches. A cast covered half his foot and went almost up to his knee. April didn't recognize the child. Probably a friend of her family's, she thought.

Colton's mother had already handed out spoons to the children who were lined up for the relay race and now gave them each a potato. This game was always a favorite with the youngsters as they tried to balance the potatoes in their spoons in a dash to the finish line.

Following Mrs. Turner's gaze, April saw Clyde urging the lone boy to come closer to his wheelchair. By the time the race started, the boy's crutches were tossed to the ground and he sat on the older man's lap, holding his own spoon and potato. The little fellow's expression had changed from a frown to one of pure glee as they were the second ones to cross the finish line.

It was a sight that touched April's heart, and a glance across the table showed that her neighbor was equally affected. For the first time since she'd known her, April saw a hint of softness on Mrs. Turner's face. Her trademark pink lips relaxed, turning ever so slightly upward, and her pale-blue eyes seemed almost dewy. The dreamy, faraway expression changed the woman's appearance so completely that she looked almost ... grandmotherly.

"Hey, April!" Steven's full-speed approach to the shelter pulled her attention away from the new facet she'd seen in her neighbor. "Colton said it's time to start getting ready for the wedding."

Almost instantly, Mrs. Turner's face hardened again, and her lips returned to their usual pursed expression. She stood to leave, and Steven came to an abrupt halt before he reached the table where April had been sitting.

"Oh," he said, his mouth grim, "I didn't realize you had Killer Bea with you." At that, he turned and stalked away.

April rose and followed Mrs. Turner to her golf cart, offering a supportive hand, only to have the gesture ignored. "Mrs. Turner, I apologize for his rudeness," she said sincerely. "Colton and I will see that he pays the consequences for it."

"Don't bother," she said, starting the motor. "I've been called worse things. As for reforming that boy, I believe you could sooner teach a pig to sing. Have a lovely wedding."

April sighed as she watched the golf cart putter away. For a while there, she'd actually thought she and Mrs. Turner were making some headway in the standing feud that seemed to be brewing between them. For a brief moment—too brief, in fact—they'd talked like neighbors instead of enemies.

And now the moment had passed for her to make peace with Mrs. Turner, although it was questionable whether the older woman wanted to make peace. April didn't like being at odds with anyone, but she felt helpless to change things.

She turned at the touch of a hand on her shoulder.

"Mrs. Turner?" Colton asked.

April nodded. "This time it's a problem with her titmice."

He pushed the hat back from his forehead and tried not to focus on the image that popped into his head. "Sounds serious. Maybe she should see a doctor."

"I don't think a doctor can fix what's ailing Bea Turner."

Nor could a doctor fix what was ailing Colton Radway. Only April possessed the cure, and he was determined that the wedding proceed according to plan.

He swallowed hard, hoping April would understand why he would stop at nothing to have her. Hoping the ends would ultimately justify his means.

"Come on," he said, nudging her toward the bathhouse. "Let's not let her or anything else ruin our special day. In another hour, you're going to be Mrs. Radway."

"I'm keeping my name."

"You can't," he insisted. "You need to do the Mr. and Mrs. thing so people will believe we're really married."

"Is that legal?"

Colton paused a moment before answering and hoped she didn't notice his hesitation. "We'll cross that bridge when we come to it." Holding the bathhouse door open for her, he said, "Your mother brought her wedding dress for you to wear."

April stopped in the open doorway. "I thought we were going to keep things casual."

"Go ahead and wear it." When she started to resist, he added, "For the same reason you need to drop Hanson and start using Radway. People expect it. Besides, it'll look nice with my tux."

April rolled her eyes. "You rented a tux for a wedding at a campground?"

Colton knew what she was thinking. That she and Eddie

hadn't gone to this much trouble for their *real* marriage eighteen years ago. And that was one more reason he wanted to make their day special.

"Don't you think that's a bit much?"

Colton propped his foot against the bathhouse door to hold it open, and he took her hand in his. "It's not every day a guy gets married," he said, feigning the part of a tearful bride. "All I'm asking for is some nice clothes to wear, a few lousy flowers, and some pictures to remember it by." He forced a dramatic sob and laid the back of his hand against his forehead. "Is that too much to ask for on the most special day of a guy's life?"

A toilet flushed, and a moment later Grandma Cole walked out. "You're a lucky girl to get such a romantic husband," she told April. "Let him have his way with the wedding, and you can have your way with him tonight."

April's eyes widened as her sweet and proper grandmother shuffled past and headed toward the camp store.

Colton grinned. "Sounds fair to me." He let go of her hand and backed away from the door. "Earl's not here yet, and nobody knows where he is. If he doesn't arrive in the next half hour, I'm going to send someone out looking for him."

With that, he dashed over to the camp store. A second later, he popped his head out to find her still staring after him. "I'll send Stella, Nicole, and Mother Joan to help you primp."

And then he was gone.

"Mother Joan?" April muttered to herself. She had to have a talk with Colton. He was taking this marriage scheme far too seriously.

By the time she was showered and dressed in the gown that had seen the marriages of her mother and niece, there was still no sign of Earl. By now, all the guests had arrived. Those who knew Earl well were speculating that he'd forgotten about the wedding or, at the very least, gotten lost along the way.

The game room had been set up for the reception. A tall, tiered cake, made by their television-chef friend Jillian, towered over plates of ham biscuits, Danish wedding cookies, mints, and peanuts on a folding table. Her friends Lanie and Nixie helped finish setting up the refreshments and decorations. Since Maybelline had taken a strong interest in the refreshments, someone had led her outside to her doghouse. And now Aunt Charlotte was whisking curious children out of the room.

April peeked outside at the picnic shelter where earlier she'd sat talking with Mrs. Turner. While she'd dressed in her wedding finery, the men had removed the picnic tables and set up folding chairs on the concrete floor. Crepe ribbons and accordion paper bells festooned the rafters.

If this were a real wedding, April couldn't have asked for a nicer one. Or a more beautiful day. There was nothing fancy about the planned ceremony. Most of the guests would be wearing the same shorts and tank tops they had donned for the reunion activities. The whole affair was simple and unpretentious, just like her and Colton.

She felt a twinge of guilt that it all amounted to a huge pretense. But there was nothing make believe about the hearty congratulations and well wishes she and Colton had received from their family and friends. April was not a person to lie, and this deception did not sit well with her.

"Don't worry," said Colton's friend Boone Shelton. "I'm sure Earl will show up soon, and you'll be married without a hitch."

April smiled, thinking about the irony in the man's words. *Married without a hitch.* That was exactly what she wanted.

Wasn't it?

She picked up the train of her gown and slung it over one

arm to prevent barefooted children from stepping on it as they weaved in and out among the impatient adults.

Maybe it's a sign, she thought. If Earl didn't show up, she could easily and gracefully put an end to this farce by refusing to reschedule it. She ought to have her head examined for considering such a foolish idea in the first place. Colton was usually the one to bail her out of unfortunate predicaments. This was the first time he'd ever talked her *into* one.

"Hey, get out of here," Nicole protested behind her. "You're not supposed to see the bride before the wedding."

Colton waved away her objections. "I thought I saw a car coming. It might be Earl's."

Many of the guests rushed to the windows, and a few stepped outside to watch the plume of dust grow closer as the car approached. But, as for April, her eyes were fixed on Colton.

She'd never seen him look so handsome as he did now in the perfectly fitted tuxedo. Accustomed to seeing him in a work shirt and jeans or shorts, she let her eyes feast on the classic elegance he emanated today.

It was obvious he'd tried to comb his hair into submission. His face was clean and tanned, marred only by a small razor nick along his jaw. The cut of the tux emphasized the broadness of his shoulders, and the royal blue cummerbund served to showcase his flat abdomen.

It could have been April's imagination, but he actually seemed taller than usual today.

"It's Earl," Joan announced when the car was close enough to identify.

A cheer went up from the crowd as the magistrate stepped out of his car and came inside.

"Some idiot deputy stopped me," her cousin told them by way of greeting. "For going five miles over the speed limit."

Colton and April looked at each other. "Deputy Dugg," they said in unison.

"Yeah, that was his name. I told him I was on my way to perform a wedding. He asked whose wedding, and when I gave him your names, he wrote me a ticket!"

He patted his pants' pockets, then his shirt, and pulled out a pair of bifocals that he perched on his nose. Her cousin, though only five years older than she, was already condemned to wearing the glasses of the middle-aged, April noted. She rubbed the brown spot on her hand that was already turning darker under the springtime sun and gave thanks that she would be starting the family she wanted so much while there was still time left.

"He even had the nerve to say something about making his quota," Earl continued.

Yep, that was definitely Alexander Dugg.

"Well, enough of that," said Joan with less than a full dose of sympathy for his plight. "Let's get on with the wedding."

Mrs. Radway and Joan herded the guests out to the picnic shelter amid the grumbled protests of a couple of kids who didn't want to leave the air-conditioned building.

Out of habit of several years, Colton grabbed his Stetson hat and placed it on his head. Then, although it was probably against some rule of weddings, he took her hand and walked with her out to the picnic shelter. They waited together at the back of the group while everyone got seated.

Still holding April's hand, he turned to her. He'd seen this dress on Nicole the previous year, but he didn't remember it looking so feminine or so small. The nipped waistline emphasized the gentle curve of April's bosom and hips. It was all he could do to keep from tracing its outline with the palms of his hands.

The veil framed her tanned face, emphasizing her large eyes that seemed to be glimmering with moisture.

"Having second thoughts?" he asked.

When she shook her head, the veil worked loose from her hair, and Colton reattached it with a white hairpin. "Me, neither," he said, smoothing the veil and then resting his hands on her shoulders. "It seems I've been waiting my whole life for this moment."

April blinked. "Buddy, if I didn't know better, I'd think you sounded like a real groom."

She nervously cleared her throat, and Colton realized he'd said too much. Perhaps it was guilt nibbling at his conscience, but he had to tell her before the ceremony.

"April, I want you to know that I'm not just doing this as a favor to you." His mouth suddenly went dry, and he licked his lips. "I care for you very much, and—"

"I know," she said, stopping him from going further. "You're doing it for the campground." She didn't meet his eyes. "Don't worry, Buddy. I won't forget that this is an arrangement ... for *both* of us."

"No, that's not what I—"

"It's okay," she insisted. "I understand."

That was the problem. She *didn't* understand. The hell with subtlety—he may as well just blurt it out.

"April, I love you, and I want you to marry me." He doubted she'd misunderstand that. But, to make sure, he added, "For real."

She smiled, the expression touching every feature of her face. "I love you, too, Buddy, and I certainly intend to marry you. For real."

She had spoken the words louder than necessary, and now she leaned toward him to give him a quick hug. When she spoke again, her lips near his ear, her words came in a whisper.

"Nice acting. You're quite believable."

Not believable enough, unfortunately.

When she pulled away from him, she nodded to the front of their makeshift chapel.

A couple of Colton's friends from college had brought a banjo and guitar and were plucking out "Close to You" with a bluegrass twang.

Earl was saying something to Steven, who waved for Colton to come join him. April's father took her hand from her faux fiancé's with a whispered comment to Colton. "I think that's your cue."

April smiled up at her father, glad that he and her mother had set aside their differences for the day. Stella and Nicole positioned themselves in front of them. They'd taken it upon themselves to shop for coordinating sundresses for the event. April had to admit the overall effect was quite romantic. And very believable. It was enough to give her very real wedding-day jitters.

Colton's friends started the processional with their stringed instruments, and her sister and niece began their walk up the aisle.

Her father tucked her arm in his. "I'm so happy for you, honey," he said. "Colton's a good man. He'll do right by you."

And once again April felt guilty for deceiving her loved ones. Before she could change her mind, the pickers changed to "Here Comes the Bride," alternating between them in the style of "Dueling Banjos."

How appropriate, she thought as her emotions dueled within her.

Her father started down the aisle, and April felt her panic rise. She was halfway there when she looked up and saw Colton watching her. Steven reached up to take the hat off the groom's head and placed it on an empty chair at the front. She almost laughed at Colton's startled reaction to the best man's unexpected move, and she was relieved to find herself feeling much more relaxed. Once again, she thanked her lucky stars to have such a good friend that he was willing to make this sacrifice for her.

Once her father passed her off to Colton, the ceremony went smoothly. Her make-believe bridegroom seemed as nervous as if this wedding were actually real, and April noticed that her knees shook when Earl asked if anyone objected to the wedding. She was half expecting someone to stand up and declare them frauds. Colton seemed to understand, and he squeezed her hand in his.

When they had said their vows, Earl pronounced them husband and wife, and Colton kissed her. As he lowered his head to hers, he whispered so low that she almost missed it. "My wife."

With all the practice they'd had at the bridal shower, April thought she would have been used to his kisses by now. But this time was somehow different ... and more special. It was ever so tender, and he held her in his arms with a sort of reverence. Even though she consciously knew it was all an act, it still made her feel treasured and precious. With her arms looped around his neck as she returned his kiss, April was overcome with the feeling that this couldn't have been a better wedding if it were legitimate.

"Oh, no! Rocky!" Jasmine cried.

At the sound of squeals and chairs scraping, the spell of the kiss was broken. Both of them turned around to see what all the commotion was about.

A furry gray blur bounded from person to person, ricocheting off shoulders and heads as skillfully as if he were leaping from treetop to treetop, the red leash dragging behind him. In his wake, women scrambled out of their seats, and men and children swung their arms in an attempt to stop the little dynamo. Unfortunately, that only fueled Rocky's attempts to evade them.

Matters got worse a moment later at the arrival of Maybelline who, with barks of delight, joined the fray.

Colton helped subdue the dog while April ran after the squirrel. But the furry fellow seemed further agitated by her flowing veil. Whipping the headpiece off, April tossed it to her sister and proceeded to tree the creature on a support beam of the picnic shelter.

Once he was safely in her arms, she cuddled the frightened animal to her chest.

Colton returned a moment later after having secured Maybelline to the doghouse. He lightly stroked the squirrel's head and then slipped an arm around April's waist. The banjo and guitar cued the guests to return to their seats as April and Colton marched down the aisle together.

April glanced up at the man beside her and saw that he was nonchalant about the disturbance.

He caught her gaze and flashed her a warm smile. "Looks like our marriage is off to a 'Rocky' start."

❦   7   ❦

Arocky start didn't begin to describe it.

First, a bee was attracted to the hairspray that April was unaccustomed to wearing. When Jasmine had tried to swat it away from her hair, the agitated insect had stung April on the cheek.

Then, as most of the guests were leaving, Colton's uncle Al had taken his hearing aid out and couldn't remember where he'd left it. Colton, April, and the remaining guests had spent more than an hour searching for it, only to have Uncle Al discover it in his shirt pocket.

And, of course, Deputy Dugg couldn't resist giving them a wedding present...a ticket for littering when the soda cans someone tied to the back of their car broke loose on the road.

And now, when they'd finally reached their hotel room after two and a half hours of driving and April was ready to claim one of the beds as her own, they opened the door to discover only one bed. A king-size bed.

"We're going to have to move to another room," she said after they set their luggage down. "I'll call the front desk."

"No." Colton took the receiver from her hand and put it back on the phone. "If we change rooms, they'll charge a different rate, and your mother will know about it when she gets her credit card receipt."

He was right. April looked around the room, but there was no sofa for one of them to sleep on. Besides the dresser and nightstand, there was a small round table with two upholstered chairs. She searched through her purse until she came up with a quarter.

"Call it," she said. "Heads or tails?"

"What are you doing?"

"Trying to decide who sleeps on the floor tonight."

"I don't think so." He caught the quarter as it spun in the air and pocketed it. "I'm not sleeping on the floor, and neither are you."

"Fine," she said, pulling the covers back. "I hope you're comfortable in the chair."

She could feel him watching her. She was already nervous about this setup, and his steady scrutiny was making it even worse. He stepped closer, and she tried to ignore him. Tried to ignore the tightness in her chest.

He stilled her hands with his own and turned her toward him. "We can sleep together in this bed," he told her calmly. "It's no big deal."

"Buddy—"

"We're lifelong best friends. We know each other better than anyone else knows either of us. Heck, we've even seen each other topless."

April smiled at the memory. At preschool they used to splash together in the wading pool, and sometimes more than their shirts would come off. "Things have changed since then," she reminded him.

She was aware of his gaze roaming over her body and, for some strange reason that she couldn't explain, it excited her.

"They definitely have," he concurred.

The same could be said for him. But standing this close to the bed, she thought it would be wiser not to focus on the way the soft curly hairs peeked out the top of his shirt.

Or the way he looked at her with those light-brown eyes that sometimes seemed to hold a touch of green. Or the way she could feel both the strength and the gentleness in his hands.

"You're right," she said. "I'm being silly. There's no reason we can't both sleep in this big bed."

While Colton pulled off his shirt, she distracted herself by going to the closet for an extra blanket, which she rolled into a long tube and placed in the center of the bed as a divider. He kicked off his pants, exposing the new scar above his knee, and April had a devil of a time keeping her eyes above his waist. His very lean, very firm waist.

Her resolve weakened, and she took a quick peek. Boxers. Navy blue with tiny red squiggles on them. Cotton, probably. She wasn't surprised. If she'd given it any thought, she would have figured him for a boxers type of guy. Comfortable, nothing fancy ... the type you keep around for a long time. Just like him.

When he moved to get into bed, he lifted the top end of the rolled blanket. His eyebrows drew together as he met her gaze. "Are you afraid of me, April?"

"No, um, of course not."

"Then why do you need this?"

She wasn't sure she knew the answer. Could it be that she was afraid of herself? Afraid that she'd wake up in the morning, her body entwined with his, and find that she liked it? Afraid that she'd go back on her vow not to mess up another friendship by throwing romance into the relationship?

She picked up the blanket from the bed and tossed it to

the floor. This pretend marriage was going to be harder than she thought. "I guess we can get by without it."

It would be awkward, but she'd manage.

Undoing the latch on her suitcase, April reached for her own nightwear. Loose shorts and a baggy, oversize T-shirt.

There were the tailored shorts she'd packed and a couple of tops, but nothing suitable for sleeping in. Although knew she had set them on top, she checked the side pockets just to make sure. No luck.

"What's the matter?"

"I can't find my pajamas."

"Did you check all of the compartments?"

"No, of course not. That's why I'm standing here wondering where my pajamas are." Immediately, April regretted taking out her frustration on Colton. He'd only been trying to help, and she'd practically snapped his head off. "I'm sorry, I didn't mean that."

"It's okay. I hear a lot of brides get cranky on their wedding night."

Throwing the covers back, he rose to his knees and fumbled through the clothes in her suitcase. Clad only in the boxers, his body was a sight to behold. April said a silent prayer of thanks that he hadn't decided to sleep in the nude. Something crinkled in his hands, and he pulled out a small folded object wrapped in tissue paper.

"What's this?" he asked, pulling away the tissue paper.

The room filled with the scent of roses—Stella's favorite perfume—and the white negligee fell onto the bed. A slip of paper landed beside it. April reached for it, but Colton got it first.

"*Happy baby making*," he read out loud. "*Love, Stella*."

He grinned, and April felt her face grow warm.

"You told her."

"She's the only one. I know she'll keep our arrangement a secret."

He said nothing ... just nodded as he rubbed the slick fabric of the nightgown between his fingers.

"I—I don't know where she got the idea that we'd—" She paused, wondering how to phrase this tactfully. "I mean, I explained to her that it would all be taken care of at the clinic."

Colton hesitated. He was tempted to just say what was on his mind, but considering how skittish she was tonight, he knew he'd best phrase his words carefully.

"Why bother with the middleman?" he said at last, attempting to keep his tone casual. "I know the procedure. And I'm sure you do, too, since you've been married before."

Of course, he tried not to focus on the latter part of his statement. He considered the time of her marriage to Eddie to be his "dark years." But now, at long last, things were starting to look up.

He just hoped they stayed that way ... especially after she found out what he'd done. He'd tried everything else, but April had steadfastly refused to see him as anything other than a friend. But now... Colton gave a mental shrug. He wouldn't think about how she might react to the news he'd eventually have to break to her. There would be time to worry about that problem later.

Right now, however, her eyes looked as large as tractor tires. "But that wasn't our arrangement," she said in a tight voice. "You said you would be willing to, you know, donate. But we agreed—"

"It's totally up to you," he said, trying to act as if it didn't matter a whit to him. "I just thought you could put the money aside for the kid's college fund. I hear fertility treatments can get very expensive, especially if you have to give it several tries."

Yes, indeed, he'd be willing to give it as many tries as it took, and then some more for good measure.

She backed away from the bed, and Colton tried not to smile at her action. "You don't have to decide right now," he told her, putting his pants back on. "Why don't you think about it while you get dressed for bed? Meanwhile, I'll run down the hall and get some ice for your bee sting."

When he was gone from the room, April stumbled to the bathroom and splashed water on her face.

Nothing in their setup was going the way she'd planned. All she wanted was one little baby, for crying out loud, and everything was blowing up in her face.

As for Colton, she didn't know what had gotten into him. He was actually *serious* about his suggestion. What was he thinking? They'd known each other for so long, they were almost like brother and sister.

"That's sick," April said out loud to her reflection in the mirror. On the other hand, if they really were like brother and sister, then why had she enjoyed his kisses so much? And why had she noticed that the hairs on his chest whorled in a counterclockwise direction? Worse, why had she wanted to brush her hand over them and feel their softness?

Her libido was in overdrive. Yes, that must be it. She was sex-crazed. For the past several years, she'd thrown all her energy into working at the campground, and now that she was alone with a handsome man, her hormones had mutinied and taken control of her brain.

Of course, if that were the case, then why hadn't she reacted like this with other men? She'd had dates, and they weren't all losers. There'd been two or three who had plenty in the looks and intelligence departments, and they'd certainly shown an interest in dancing the horizontal mambo with her. But for some reason, April had never worked up any enthusiasm over any of her dates.

She slipped her clothes off and pulled the white night-gown over her head. Putting her hands on her hips, she turned and examined herself in the mirror. It was a good color for her and served to play up the varying shades of blonde streaks in her hair. As for the cut, it couldn't have fit better. The simple design even managed to make her look a whole cup size larger.

Not that it mattered, April hastily reminded herself. It was just for sleeping in.

The shimmery fabric seemed to caress her body where it flowed over dips and curves. It still smelled of roses. Her sister had overanticipated April's and Colton's fondness for one another, she decided. But that wasn't reason enough for her to get all worked up tonight. Even so, April impulsively slid a peach gloss lipstick over her lips.

"Sunburn," she said, as if trying to convince herself there was no other reason for doing so. But she had to admit, the overall effect really looked good.

Colton had looked good, too. April brushed her hair into its usual loose, swingy style. And he'd made an excellent point about setting up a college fund for the baby.

Maybe, she thought, she ought to consider all aspects of his suggestion before deciding it was not an option. And perhaps if she took advantage of his offer, she could get this unexpected case of passion out of her system.

She opened the bathroom door as he was returning with a bucket of ice. He hadn't bothered to put a shirt on, and April wondered how many female heads he'd turned as he walked down the long hall and back.

He closed the door, never bothering to take his eyes off her. His gaze slowly traveled the length of her, lingering at her face, her waist, her legs, and then traveling back up to her eyes. April suddenly felt self-conscious, a feeling she wasn't accustomed to having with her best friend.

"It, uh, fits well," he said at last. He turned away from her to set the ice bucket on the bench in the entryway, but April could have sworn that he held the cold container to his bare chest first.

When he faced her again, he held a chip of ice in his hand.

"Does your face still hurt?"

She'd forgotten all about the bee sting, but she found herself nodding yes.

He brushed her hair aside and touched the ice to her cheek, holding it in place by bracing his fingers against her skin.

Unable to meet his gaze, April looked straight ahead, her eyes level with the top of his chest. Small beads of moisture, presumably from the ice bucket, clung to his torso and the strands of brown that covered it.

After a moment, he removed the ice and wiped a thumb across the affected area. "That should be enough for now," he said. "Too much of the cure can be worse than the ailment."

A naughty thought came to mind as April imagined the cure for what else had been ailing her. She gave herself a mental shake. *Enough of that!*

"It's been a long day," she said, stepping away from the deadly cure in front of her. "I think I'll go to sleep now."

Like a frightened rabbit, she hopped into the bed, switched off the light, and hid under the covers. The mattress jostled as he slid in on the other side and adjusted the covers around him.

"Good night, Buddy," she whispered.

She heard him sigh, and then he scooted closer. April held her breath, wondering whether he was just hogging the bed or had something else in mind.

"April?"

"What, Buddy?"

"I enjoyed our wedding today."

She smiled at the memory of their special day. Despite some minor inconveniences, it had gone very well. "Me, too."

"And I'd never seen Clyde grin so wide as he did when you asked him to dance with you."

April remembered their friend's pleased response when she sat on the arm of his wheelchair and danced a slow one with him. It hadn't even ruined their fun when her gown got caught in the wheel spokes. Thinking of all the others she'd danced with today, she flexed the stiffness from her tired calf muscles.

"Did you see Steven teaching me some of the newest steps?"

She was aware of Colton nodding in response.

Under the sheet, he laced his fingers with hers. He cleared his throat. "There's something I want to ask you."

She forced herself to breathe. Most likely he was going to press her for an answer on his earlier suggestion, and she still hadn't come to a decision. "Yes?"

"I want to kiss you good night."

"You do?" she squeaked.

He chuckled. The sound of it was deep and, for the first time, a little bit unnerving.

"I do." He paused. "Is this deja vu, or haven't I already said this once today?"

He leaned closer, fumbling for her in the dark, then touched her chin to turn her face toward him.

In the next moment, before she could decide whether to register a protest or urge him closer, his mouth covered hers. April braced her hands against his shoulders. Of their own volition, her fingers clutched the rounded muscles of his arms. But instead of pushing him away, they traced the curve upward and explored the line of his collarbones down to the hollow where they met. Once there, she was rewarded with the tickly softness of that enticing counter-clockwise swirl.

She arched her neck as his hand slid behind her head and began a slow, steady massage that smoothed away all tightness and dissolved any remaining resistance.

"April, honey," he murmured against her lips.

"Mmm."

"Let me give you a baby." He kissed her again. "Now."

"I suppose..." She returned his kiss, feeling drugged by his very nearness. "...that would be all right."

His head dipped as he kissed her neck and trailed down to where the nightgown parted in the front. April rolled to one side, and the movement brought her closer to the length of him.

Colton's arm went around the small of her back, bringing her so close that she couldn't move if she wanted to ... which she didn't.

"April, there's something I have to tell you first," Colton murmured against her ear.

She nodded, taking great pleasure in the moist warmth of his breath on her neck.

"This baby is going to have a real father."

"I know, Buddy," she assured him. "I have no doubt you'll always be there for this child."

She knew he would be there for the baby—and for her—long after their arrangement ended. And she thought it was sweet of him to remind her of it at this particular time.

"No, I mean the baby is going to have a *legitimate* father."

April could have sworn that the almost imperceptible tightening of his grip on her back had nothing to do with passion.

"What are you trying to say, Buddy?"

He took a slow, deep breath, and April mentally braced herself. This was what he always did when he had bad news for her. "Remember how your college friend's father couldn't perform the marriage on the campus grounds because the law only allowed him to marry people in his own district?"

April felt herself tense. Oh, no, please don't let it be what she thought it might be.

"Well, your cousin Earl happened to mention that the law has changed in the years since then." He paused a moment, as if waiting for her reaction before telling her the rest. But she was too stunned to react. "He's now licensed to marry people anywhere in the State of Virginia."

The tightness in April's throat threatened to paralyze her voice. "You mean, we're really married? It wasn't a mock wedding?"

"Right on both counts."

"Why didn't you tell me this sooner?" she asked and was annoyed by the shrillness in her voice.

"I tried to, but—"

"Why did you wait until now?"

She heard him suck air between his teeth and knew she wouldn't like this news any better than the last.

"Because then you wouldn't have married me."

"You knew *before* the wedding? You sneaky son of a—" She tried to take a swing at him, but when her arm remained pinned at her side, she suddenly understood why he'd held her so tightly. Thwarted there, she tried to kick him, but her legs were pinned between his.

"April, honey, I told you this because I want you to be my wife ... in the fullest sense of the word."

It was all Colton could do to keep her from hauling off and whacking him. He supposed he deserved it, what with tricking her into a real marriage. She hadn't taken him seriously when he had given her his heart and asked her out on dates. Now, when he was offering her his body as well as his heart, he had to know that she was accepting him as a wife accepts a husband.

She was small, but the long hours of working outdoors had made her as strong as a hardened athlete. When she quit struggling in his arms, he loosened his hold on her, and she began her attack anew.

"We made a deal," she protested, "and you *tricked* me!"

To protect the freshly healed wound above his knee—as well as other valuable assets—Colton slid out of the bed and felt a pillow hit him upside the head. He flipped the light switch on so he could see her in case she got the notion to throw something heavier.

And it was a good thing he did. First came the notepad from the nightstand. Fortunately, her aim was bad, and it hit the wall behind him. Next was the list of places to visit in the area. Her aim was better this time, but he managed to dodge the travel book.

Considering her reaction, she was taking the news better than he'd anticipated.

Now she picked up the hardback Gideon Bible. That one could hurt.

"Uh, April, I don't think that's a good idea."

Looking down at the book in her hand, she seemed undecided for a moment before putting it back in the drawer. Colton breathed a sigh of relief. But the cease-fire was short-lived. She picked up the TV remote control and hurled it toward his midsection.

"Why did you lie to me?"

He didn't say anything. He was wondering how long it would take before she noticed the alarm clock and threw that, too.

It seemed as though her energy was spent. She sat on the edge of the bed, her head in her hands, looking defeated. "Buddy, why did you trick me into marrying you?"

"Uh—" What could he say to that? The obvious thing to say—the truth—was that he was in love with her. He'd tried to get her attention before, but she thought he was joking when he asked her to go out with him. He had considered telling her about the change in the law before the wedding, but at the time it had seemed like the perfect solution to get the two of them together. He'd anticipated that if they were really married, she'd be forced to see him more as a husband and lover than a friend, and that eventually she would come to love him as much as he loved her. In his fantasy, he'd imagined her wanting to *stay* married to him.

But he couldn't tell her that. If he did, she'd be out of here quicker than a raccoon could raid a garbage can. So, instead, he told her what she wanted to hear.

He sat down beside her on the bed, taking care not to spook her with an inadvertent touch.

"I didn't want to take a chance that you'd go back to your original plan," he said, "if you didn't get pregnant right away."

She looked up at him, her eyes showing more tiredness than could be attributed to their busy day.

Colton reached over and took her hand in his. "I need you, April." He'd spooked her. She tried to pull away from him, but he wouldn't let her. "At the campground. There's no way I could hire someone to do all that you do."

Although she seemed somewhat appeased by his answer, she most definitely was not pleased. And if he'd had any doubt about that, the rolled-up blanket in the middle of the bed that night let him know exactly what she thought of his trickery.

8

April paced up and down the length of the sandy beach surrounding the Cozy Acres lake. Many of the children had been working on their sandcastles for an hour or more, and each sought to win the prize of a beach bucket full of candy for his or her creation. As the sole judge in this competition, she was being bombarded by children urging her to look at their masterpieces.

School had let out for the summer a couple of days ago, and April was grateful for the heightened workload as she launched into her role as campground activities director. Staying busy helped keep her from thinking about being married. *Really* married.

She hadn't been able to stay angry with Colton, which made matters worse. If only she'd been able to remain rip-roaring mad at him, this whole situation would be easier to deal with. But, instead, she'd found this time with Colton the most fun of her life. It was a pleasure to wake up and see the face of her best friend first thing every morning. And it was refreshing to have someone share the lonely evenings with her.

Although she'd originally declined to make love with Colton because she hadn't wanted to mess up their impending divorce by consummating the union, it was now more a matter of shyness. Her inhibitions had been loosened on their wedding night, thanks to the postnuptial champagne toasts, but since then she'd worried about the consummation of their vows until she felt frozen stiff. All these years she'd shared everything with him ... her hopes, sorrows, joys, and special occasions. But she'd never shared her body with him, and suddenly her best friend seemed like a stranger.

"Miss April." A small hand tugged at the hem of her shirt. April looked down to see six-year-old Rachel's enormous blue eyes staring up at her. "David said he's going to crash my castle with a wrecking ball."

April glanced in the direction the girl pointed just in time to see the middle child of the three siblings roll an overinflated beach ball all-too-innocently toward his younger brother. She strolled over to David and knelt to his eye level.

"You know," she said gently. "If I were you, I'd be *helping* Rachel with her sandcastle. Because, if she wins, she just might share the prize with you."

He shrugged in apparent unconcern. "I can get candy of my own."

It seemed as though the impending payoff of watching his sister's sandcastle crumble was more enticing than the iffy possibility of sharing her winnings.

But the youngest of the Morgan children thought differently. Jason jumped up from sitting on the beach, his trunks weighted with sand, and ran to Rachel. "I'll help you," he said, suddenly full of enthusiasm for the project.

Fearing the structure wouldn't be standing much longer, April took a long look and committed it to memory, then snapped a picture with her cell phone. Just in case.

A while later, Rachel's castle still intact, April awarded the prizes. The bucket of candy went to an older girl who'd made a three-tiered design. Seeing the crestfallen look on Rachel's face, April gave her and Jason each a coupon for a free candy bar at the camp store. And then she gave suckers as consolation prizes to all the rest who entered.

"Softy," Steven said beside her.

She turned and handed her young employee one of the remaining suckers. "When you own the campground," she said smugly, "you can make whatever rules you want."

Steven pocketed the sucker for later. April supposed it wasn't considered "cool" for a sixteen-year-old to eat a lollipop in public.

A scream split the air and was followed immediately by giggles of delight. Fearing that someone might be hurt, she sought the source of the noise. Mr. Morgan got up from his folding lounge chair and walked toward his three children. He didn't seem to be in a hurry, so it must not have been anything serious, she surmised. And then she saw Rachel's sandcastle.

David stood triumphantly over the misshapen structure, an empty plastic pail in his hand. Water dripped from the container, and it was plain to see that he'd "melted" the sandcastle. A tear-faced Rachel sobbed the story to her father while pointing between her creation and her brother. Little Jason patted his big sister on the arm.

Oddly enough, the scene made April think of her misbegotten marriage to Colton. Like the sandcastle, their union was only meant for show. It would soon dissolve, and as Rachel and Jason had discovered, the arrival of a third party would bring an end to what they'd put together. In April and Colton's case, that third party would also be a child.

And for reasons she couldn't understand, it saddened her.

She didn't know what magic words he'd spoken, but for now, Mr. Morgan had brought peace to his clan. Rachel moved to a spot farther away from the water and began building a new castle, this time joining forces with the girl who'd won the candy.

April supposed that someday she, too, would build a new relationship with someone else. Such a shame, she thought, because she rather liked that first sandcastle.

"You got any iodine?" Steven asked.

"Sure," she said, still shaken by her musings. "Did you cut yourself?"

He shook his head. "Clyde caught it on the arm when Rocky didn't want to go back into the pet carrier." Steven paused a moment while April took in the implication. "It's time, April."

Leaving the children to their parents' care, April walked with Steven back to the camp store. She'd been putting this off. From the start, she'd intended to return Rocky to the wild. She just hadn't thought it would be so soon. And she was having a hard time letting go.

Steven nudged her with his elbow. "He'll be okay," he assured her. "You did a good job of teaching him to find nuts and stuff."

He opened the camp store door for her to go inside first. Steven was right. Rocky shouldn't have much trouble finding food. She had taken the leashed squirrel on numerous excursions out to the woods where she'd shown him how to find acorns. And Steven had been grossed out when she allowed Rocky to climb the lower branches of the catalpa tree to scavenge for caterpillars.

Clyde sat behind the counter, glaring at the blue plastic pet carrier positioned at the far end of it. Both of his arms, from the bottom of his short sleeves to the backs of his hands, showed angry red scratches. "Your squirrel is going squirrelly."

April got the first aid kit from the storage closet and set it down beside Clyde, then she began cleaning the wounds. "Did he bite you?"

"Nah." Clyde winced once as she tended one of the deeper scratches. "Nipped my finger, but he didn't break the skin."

She smiled in relief. She didn't think there was any risk of rabies, but bite wounds could easily become infected. By the time she finished dabbing Clyde's arms with the red iodine, he looked like he'd been in a fight with a she-bear. And lost.

Walking to the end of the counter, she picked up the pet carrier. The battle with Clyde must have tired Rocky out, for he now lay curled in a ball on his bed of towels.

"Can I go with you?" Steven asked.

April nodded, and Steven took the carrier from her.

"Hey, wait a minute," Clyde called as they were leaving. He pulled out a bag from behind the counter. "Here's a going-away present for the rat."

A bag of unsalted peanuts in the shell. Clyde's own personal stash. She flashed him a smile as she accepted the offering on Rocky's behalf. Clyde was not a man to hold grudges.

"Where are we taking him?" Steven asked once they were outside.

"Back to that oak tree where I first found him."

He nodded his approval. "That's far enough away from the campers that he won't be bothering them for food."

They were crossing the open field where just three weeks ago they'd played softball at her family reunion. Colton climbed down from where he'd been tightening bolts on the swing set and called out a greeting.

Steven set the carrier down and ran over to tell him what they were doing. Colton packed his tools in the small pickup truck he drove around the campground, and April felt a sense of relief when he joined them.

He knelt in front of Rocky and stuck a finger in the cage door to scratch the animal's shoulder. "So, you're moving into your own place, huh? Be careful," he warned. "It's a jungle out there."

As he stood, he pushed the cowboy hat back and rubbed his forehead. "I think Rocky'll be fine," he announced. Then, to Steven, he added, "But I'm not too sure about his *m-o-t-h-e-r*," spelling out the last word.

"His mother will do just fine," April assured them both. But, although she wouldn't admit it to the males who accompanied her, she was reluctant to turn Rocky loose in the wild. What if he got in a fight with a bigger, older squirrel? What if he fell from the tree? She tried to slow her breathing as they walked along the horse trail toward Rocky's birthplace. The animal was certain to pick up on her feelings, and it wouldn't do for her to make him nervous about his reentry into the wild.

They reached the oak tree much too quickly, and April stalled by giving him a peanut. When Rocky was done with the treat, she took him out of his confinement and held him close to her chest while Colton unhooked the harness. She took her time stroking her furry little friend, knowing this might be the last time she'd ever see him. April's vision blurred slightly, and her eyes filled with hot tears.

Steven reached over and patted the little fellow's head. "Let me give you a word of advice," he told the animal. "Stay out of Killer Bea's pecan tree. That woman's nothing but trouble."

April didn't have the energy to chastise Steven again for his disrespect. She'd have a talk with him later, when she wasn't so at odds with her emotions.

Colton placed a couple of peanuts where the lower limb of the tree jutted from its trunk. "Why don't you set him here until he gets his bearings?" he suggested.

Rocky was starting to squirm in her arms, so she really couldn't prolong the goodbye. With a heavy heart, she lifted him to the branch. The little ingrate ignored the peanuts and promptly scooted up to a higher perch in the tree.

"Lucky guy," said Steven.

Surprised by the comment, April turned toward him.

He shrugged, still watching Rocky. "He's got his freedom."

If April's heart hadn't already been on the verge of breaking, it was in shards now.

"Oh, Steven," she said, placing a comforting arm around the boy's lanky shoulders. She'd grown very fond of the boy in these short months, and though she would miss him terribly when he finished his stint at the youth facility, she wanted him to make a place for himself. And she feared that his run-ins with Mrs. Turner were only hurting his chance for a successful transition back into society.

Steven was clearly uncomfortable with April's gushing. With another shrug of his shoulders, he pulled away from her.

"I've gotta go finish mowing." With a quick salute to the squirrel, he was gone.

She didn't have time to fret about Steven before she saw something plummet from the tree to her feet. Her heart gave a lurch.

"Relax," said Colton, moving to stand beside her. "It's only a twig with some dead leaves on it."

They stood side by side, peering up into the branches of the tree. The squirrel had moved even higher and hidden himself behind the large green leaves. At least he knew not to make himself an open target to hawks and such.

"I can't help it," April confessed. "I'm going to worry about him, no matter what."

Colton turned his attention away from the tree and

focused his brown eyes on April. "We've raised him the best we know how. The rest is up to him."

"But what if he has trouble adapting to the wild? What if he can't find enough food?"

Her husband tossed the remainder of the peanuts around the base of the tree. "If he needs us, we'll be here for him."

"What if he's lonely and misses us?"

Shoving the empty bag into his pocket, he put his arm around her shoulders, much as she'd tried to do with Steven to offer some measure of comfort. But April didn't resist the gesture. She leaned against him, grateful for the bit of strength he was able to convey to her through his mere touch.

"He'll find a female," Colton said, his voice soft and sure.

April felt her lower lip go out in a childish pout. "They probably won't even invite us to the wedding."

"As long as they love each other, that's all that matters." He was talking about the squirrel, April knew, but his message seemed much more intimate.

"Suppose she's not good enough for him?" she asked petulantly. It was ridiculous, her talking about a squirrel as if he were her son going off to make his mark in the world, but she couldn't help herself. She was taking this very personally.

Colton squeezed her shoulder, and she was aware that his body had tensed.

"Am I good enough for you, April?"

What an odd question. She looked up at Colton, wondering what had prompted such a query. "You're my best friend, Buddy. Always have been, always will be."

And she was determined to keep that promise, no matter what. Her statement was a reminder to hurry and settle her awkwardness with him so she could get pregnant and let them both get on with their old, comfortable relationship of being "just friends."

"That's not what I'm talking about," he persisted. His words carried an extra weight of meaning.

April felt herself blush. "Oh, you mean—" He must have been referring to his suitability as the father of her child. There was no question about that. "Well, of course," she began with hesitation. "You're smart. You have a great personality. Physically, you're in great shape."

They were all traits that she wanted her child to inherit.

Colton gnashed his teeth. Using the excuse of searching for Rocky, he stepped away from April and peered up into the leaves. If she thought he was that wonderful, then why wouldn't she let him make love to her? Better yet, why wouldn't she let him love her?

He'd hoped that, by her playing the role of his wife, it would show her how much she'd been missing by ruling him out as a love interest. Unfortunately, he felt like he was just as far away from winning her over as he'd always been.

Colton unfisted his hands and shoved them into his back pockets. He'd wasted too many of his single years waiting for her to realize they were meant to be together. And he didn't intend to waste their married time together, waiting for her to realize she loved him, too.

He felt the muscles in his neck and shoulders relax as he contemplated the fact that she *did* love him. She might not admit it at this point—or worse, she might say she loved him as a best friend—but she did, indeed, love him. He was sure of that. And he was sure that, if she would only allow herself to see it, she also loved him as a wife loves a husband.

Perhaps what he needed to do was *show* her what he already knew. Let her see for herself that this pretense of mere friendship was a bigger sham than their make-believe marriage had been.

He bent and picked up the empty pet carrier. "It's time to

say goodbye to Rocky. He can't get on with his new life until he leaves the old one behind."

It was also time to say goodbye to their old ways of relating to each other. In their case, it was more a matter of not being able to leave the old life behind until they got on with the new.

That decided, he would have to lead her into their new life. Colton smiled with anticipation. This could turn out to be quite satisfying.

For both of them.

A few minutes later, Deputy Alexander Dugg leaned against the door of the truck Colton had been driving earlier. April took a step back, away from the man.

"You're trespassing, Dugg," Colton said without preamble. "I want you off my property. Now."

"I don't think so." The deputy slapped a thick pad against the palm of his hand. "I'm here on official duty."

To Dugg's obvious chagrin, Colton did not appear impressed. "My, my, aren't you just full of duty?"

The double entendre was not lost on the smaller man. April watched in amazement as Dugg turned a crimson red that had nothing to do with the hot June sun.

"It's only Friday afternoon," Colton continued. "Aren't you a little early getting started with your weekend cop job?"

April elbowed him, hoping he'd get the hint and not goad the little man into a showdown.

"Laugh if you want, but come next election I'm going to be your new sheriff." Dugg sounded like a little boy on a play-ground, trying to defend his turn in line at the sliding board. He must have noticed it, too, for he tried to project more authority into his next statement. "I understand that you two have been harboring a wild animal as a pet. *Without* a permit."

She wondered what the penalty would be for this infraction of the law. Hopefully, it wouldn't mean another trip to jail.

Colton opened his arms wide, as if he weren't aware that the pet crate was still in his possession. "I don't have a wild animal," he told the deputy. He turned ever so innocently toward April. "Do *you* have a wild animal?"

Following his lead, she shrugged and lifted her palms upward. The red leash dangled from her right hand. "I don't have a wild animal."

With a conspiratorial wink to April, he set the carrier down and took her free hand in his. "Perhaps you've been hearing about my wife," he told Dugg. "She can be quite the wild animal at times."

April didn't know which bothered her more, his innuendo or the fact that he'd called her his wife.

"Right, my *pet?*" he said, continuing his play on words.

"Um..."

The deputy glanced between the instigators standing in front of him. "Just because you're two of Bliss County's leading business owners doesn't give you the right to break the laws I'm sworn to uphold. I am not going to be lenient about this and have voters think I play favorites."

He paused as if to let the meaning of his words sink in.

"I'm charging you both with a Class Four misdemeanor, which carries a fine of up to two hundred and fifty dollars."

He had just finished writing them up when he lifted his head and sniffed the air.

"I smell smoke."

"What's the matter, Dugg? Did they raise your quota to three citations a day?" Colton chuckled as if amused by his own joke. "It's probably just your friend Mrs. Turner burning some brush."

Dugg glared at Colton, as if wishing he could find a way to silence his impertinent tongue.

April turned to her husband. "I don't think so, Buddy. Mrs. Turner always gets someone to haul it away because of her asthma."

The three of them turned as one toward the Turner property. A black plume of thick smoke rose in the air at the far edge of the campground.

"Oh, no," said April. "That's no campfire."

"It's that hoodlum again," the deputy declared. "I just know he's behind this."

He dashed to his squad car and reported an uncontrolled burning to the dispatcher. Then he motioned for them to follow him and spun out on the gravel road. April wondered if the little man pictured himself in a cape and tights with a red "*S*" on the chest.

Colton waited until only a split second after April got in the truck and closed the passenger door before roaring off after the deputy.

Fortunately, the vehicle was equipped with a large water canister for dousing lingering embers in campfires. But April knew they would need more than the few gallons they had with them. She pulled the cellular phone out of her back pocket and called the camp store. Clyde answered and said Steven was with him.

Relieved, she turned to Colton to relay the good news. "Steven's at the store. He has an alibi."

"Yep," Clyde continued, "you can be mighty proud of this boy. He's been working hard mowing the back field." April heard him talk away from the telephone as he directed his words to the teen. "You just got here. Now sit down and cool off before you go back out. No sense making yourself sick."

Sick was exactly how April felt. She'd forgotten he had headed out to finish mowing after he'd left her and Colton with the squirrel. His path would have taken him right by Mrs. Turner's property. She felt further sickened when she remembered his comment to Rocky about staying away from "Killer Bea's" pecan tree.

She hung up the phone and voiced her fears to Colton, who didn't say anything but only gritted his teeth. She could tell his concern was as great as hers. He, too, feared Steven may have set the blaze in retaliation for the elderly woman's spiteful ways.

It took them longer than she would have liked to reach the site of the fire, but Colton was driving carefully to avoid any children that might dart into the truck's path.

A row of six large green hay rolls sat along the fence that separated the campground from Mrs. Turner's well-manicured yard. Four of the rolls flamed like a bonfire, sending thick smoke into the air.

Dugg had retrieved a small, hand-held fire extinguisher from the trunk of his car and now sprayed ineffectually at the leaping flames. Mrs. Turner was making more headway with the garden hose, but the fire was smoldering deep within the hay that stood almost as tall as the deputy himself.

Colton didn't bother with the water tank in the truck bed. "The only way to put the fire out is by unrolling and then soaking the rolls."

That said, he attacked the most involved roll with a rake from the truck.

April could see that Mrs. Turner was fighting a losing battle, both with the garden hose and within herself. Tears coursed down the woman's wrinkled cheeks. "My climbing roses!" she said between choking coughs. "They're going to burn to kingdom come."

April couldn't argue about that. The dainty pink flowers

that sought their support from the rail fence were already curling under the intense heat.

"Mrs. Turner, your health is much more important than any flowers," she said, taking the green plastic hose from her neighbor's arthritis-gnarled hands. "Why don't you come with me and sit down while you catch your breath?"

Dugg continued the attack with the hose while April led the coughing woman to the house. Mrs. Turner refused to go inside where it was cool but sat on the porch where she could watch the men's progress with the fire. April retrieved her inhaler from the kitchen table, and Mrs. Turner was soon breathing easier.

A few minutes later the fire truck arrived. Drafting water from the creek where Steven had intended to swim just a few short weeks ago, the firefighters quickly contained the blaze.

"It's that boy," Mrs. Turner said as April got up to leave. "He's holding a grudge against me, and this is his way of retaliating."

She stopped at the door of the screened porch. Mrs. Turner was probably right about Steven holding a grudge against her. The anger in his voice when he'd spoken of the Killer Bea had been quite evident. But she didn't think he would intentionally risk the woman's life—or the lives of the campers at Cozy Acres—to get even with her.

At least, she *hoped* he wouldn't. "I don't know, Mrs. Turner. All I can say is I hope you're wrong."

"We'll see who's right and who's wrong," the older woman promised as April crossed the close-cropped yard in front of her. "I'm going to have the fire marshal begin an investigation."

Earlier today, Colton had sought to put out a fire. Now he was trying to start one. With April.

The problem was, she was currently focused on whether Steven had set the hay fire and what might happen to him if he had. She wasn't taking his hints. Subtlety be damned, he was going to try the direct approach.

Already showered and dressed for bed, she paced the floor near the couch where he sat. She wore the loose beige-and-brown shorts and baggy green T-shirt that her sister had hidden from her on their wedding day. Surprisingly, the sight was far from unpleasant. The shirt flowed over two small tempting hillocks and a flat abdomen before disappearing into the folded-over waistband of the shorts that were a size too large. Working at the campground, she had become as strong as any man of her height, but tonight her nightwear made her appear delicate.

The next time she paced past him, he caught her arm and pulled her down to sit beside him on the couch. "You're tense," he said, stating the obvious. "Let me help you relax."

When she was seated, he turned sideways so that she sat between his legs, and he began a slow kneading of the taut muscles around her neck and shoulders. Her head lolled back under his gentle ministrations, and he moved the massage up to her scalp where he could enjoy the silky sensation of her soft blonde curls.

"*Mmm*, Buddy, you have magic fingers."

He inhaled deeply, taking in the scent of her peach shampoo. Slow down, he told himself. Don't rush it. He forced himself to concentrate on his long-range goal. Not only did he want her in his bed for tonight, but also in his life forever.

Their first time had to be special. He wanted to show her that they weren't just making a baby; they were making *love*. He wanted her to see the love that had been growing between them since the first time they had played together in preschool. Tonight, he intended to start breaking down the barriers she had erected between them.

But he would have to play his cards very carefully. If he moved too fast, he'd frighten her away. And after all these years, he wasn't willing to risk such a loss.

April hunched and relaxed her shoulders, giving in to the mesmerizing feel of his kneading hands. What a dear friend he was, trying to calm her nerves after her upsetting day. Although he'd tried not to show it, she could tell he was reluctant to release Rocky back into the wild. And she knew he had been every bit as disturbed as she was by the fire and the possibility that Steven was involved, but he was putting her comfort before his own. She felt him lean close behind her.

"It's been three weeks," he said. "Don't you think it's time to get on with your business of making a baby?"

Her shoulders tightened again, and his strong fingers immediately rubbed away the tension.

He was right about trying to conceive now. If she became pregnant this month or next, the baby would be born in early spring, before the summer rush. Unfortunately, she felt uncomfortable about going the direct route with Colton.

She supposed she could still let the fertility clinic handle the procedure, even though it would be his child. But it did seem rather silly to waste their time and money to involve a third party when—as Colton had pointed out—they were perfectly capable of doing it themselves. She wondered if he was still interested.

She wondered if doing so would change things forever between them.

Of course it would, she chided herself. Perhaps the bigger question was, would she be able to live with the changes wrought by the introduction of sex into their friendship?

He seemed aware that she was debating her decision.

"The sooner you get pregnant," he reminded her, "the sooner you'll have the baby and be back at work."

And the sooner he could get on with his own life, she mentally finished for him. He was already inconveniencing himself for her, so it wouldn't be fair to prolong their arrangement any longer than necessary.

"You're right," she agreed. "Are you sure you want to go through with this?"

"It's a tough job," he said with a grin, "but somebody's got to do it."

They stood, and she followed him to the bedroom like a horse thief headed for the hangman's noose.

Once they were in bed, though, some of her reluctance faded. *It's natural attraction,* she reminded herself. Unfortunately, her shyness soon increased.

"Let's turn off the lights," Colton thoughtfully suggested.

Great idea. Then maybe he wouldn't see how nervous and trembly she was. On the other hand, she thought inanely, maybe her involuntary shaking would make it more pleasurable for him.

When he touched her, the trembling ceased, and she was filled with a warmth that spread all the way down to her toes. Strange how her body's reaction could be so different than that of her brain. Maybe if she just went ahead with this, she'd get these longings out of her system and fortify herself for another long period of celibacy until she found the man she would eventually marry for real.

"We don't have to rush this," Colton said. "I could just hold you for a moment."

Even though he couldn't see her response in the darkened room, she nodded. Scooting closer, she leaned into his embrace. Yes, indeed, he'd certainly changed a lot since their days of playing in the wading pool at preschool.

Tenderly, he touched her cheek, her nose, her lips, and

followed with a kiss to each spot. The touches and kisses trailed down her neck. The tingling sensation that he elicited was enough to make April forget her hesitation.

Despite her newfound enthusiasm for sharing this baby making procedure with Colton, something held her back. It was like a gnat that she couldn't see and which refused to go away.

It was almost like they were being watched.

"Buddy, did you pull the shades?"

He raised his head from kissing her neck. "Yeah, why?"

"It feels like somebody's looking at us."

He laughed and pulled her to him. "It's first-time jitters, honey."

"No, I don't think so. This is a really weird, creepy feeling."

"Thanks a lot."

"No, I'm not talking about you. It's something else, but I don't know what."

She heard him sigh as he pulled away from her to switch on the lamp. Blinking against the harsh glare of light, she searched the room for whatever might be amiss. There was nothing on Colton's side of the room, but then April's gaze fell to her edge of the bed.

Large brown eyes stared back at her and rubbery lips turned upward in a doggy smile. Golden, whiskered eyebrows lifted in alternate turns as Maybelline glanced curiously between April and Colton.

"Oh, no," she said. "Now?"

The dog shifted uneasily where it sat beside the bed.

"I think that means yes," Colton said.

Before April could push the covers back to get up, Colton dashed the golden retriever to the backyard they shared with the other residents of the duplex.

And then he returned to finish what they'd started.

❦ 9 ❦

"**C**ome on." Nicole grabbed her by the hand and pulled her into the fourth store that morning. "Let's finish what we started."

April allowed herself to be led into the aptly named Baby Store, but that didn't stop her from complaining. "Aren't you exhausted? I thought pregnant women were supposed to take naps and have people bring them snacks."

Nicole laughed, and April loved the happy sound of it. She'd be happy, too, if she were pregnant.

"Oh, don't be silly," her niece told her. "If you can put in fourteen-hour days at the campground, I know you can handle shopping for a crib with me."

It wasn't the shopping she minded so much. It was the pregnant women, and the mothers with toddlers clinging to their legs. It was the envy that ate away at the inside of her to see these lucky people preparing a special place for their little loved ones.

It had been almost a week since she and Colton had started trying to have a baby of their own, much too soon to know if they'd been successful.

What she *hadn't* been successful at doing, however, was satisfying her physical cravings. If anything, that first time with Colton had made her desire stronger. And even though she kept telling herself they were only together every night because they were trying for a baby, she couldn't deny how much she looked forward to their private time together.

And she couldn't deny how much she enjoyed waking up with her "best buddy" and sharing all aspects of her life with him.

"What do you think of this one?" Nicole pointed to an oak Jenny Lind crib outfitted with a yellow gingham and eyelet lace comforter.

"It looks like the one you saw at the last store, only it costs ten dollars more."

"Uh-uh, it's on sale—ten dollars off." Nicole's attention was drawn away from the crib when a young mother walked by with a newborn infant strapped to the front of her. "Hey, I think that's Teresa."

At the sound of her name the young woman turned, and she flashed a bright smile of recognition at Nicole. Soon the two were bringing each other up to date on the latest happenings in their lives.

"Oh, I'm sorry, I didn't introduce you. This is my Aunt April. April, Teresa and I graduated from high school together. And this little guy is Liam."

As they were saying their hellos, April noticed that the baby's position in the carrier looked uncomfortable. "I think he has his foot tucked under him."

The young woman looked down at the sleepy little one. "I've been having trouble with this thing all morning. I don't know why it's giving me so much trouble all of a sudden."

But Nicole quickly figured out the problem. "The strap is twisted. April, if you'll hold Liam, I'll help Teresa untangle this contraption."

Before she could protest that she had no experience with infants, the baby was in her arms. She worried about supporting his head properly, and she worried about dropping him. And then a thought occurred to her. If he were a puppy or an orphaned squirrel, she'd just cuddle him close to her chest. She did, and he turned his angelic face toward her, his mouth opening instinctively in search of food. It was enough to send strange, tingling sensations to her womb.

April adjusted his position so as not to confuse him into thinking it was lunchtime. She nuzzled his fuzzy blond head, enjoying the sweet, powdery smell that was common to babies. Heaven must smell like this, she thought. If not, it should.

"Hey, April, you're a natural." Nicole flashed her a smile and tugged at a buckle on the blue papoose. "Oh, I see," she declared to Teresa. "This flap was turned inside out when you put it on."

April took up a swaying motion as she watched the two younger women work out the problem. With little grunts of contentment, Liam let her know he was comfortable in her arms. She could get used to this quite easily, she noted happily.

"I should have known Will would have something to do with this," Teresa complained. "Ever since we brought Liam home from the hospital, he has been doing everything wrong. You know, I don't think he listened to a thing they taught us in prenatal class."

"They have classes on how to use baby equipment?" By now, April was jouncing Liam in a gentle up and down movement.

"Not exactly. The hospital offers a course on the basics for first-timers like us. They show you how to diaper your baby, give him a bath ... stuff like that."

Nicole threaded the strap back through the buckle and

pulled it snug. "Will will get the hang of things," she said. "He probably just needs a little time and practice."

"Practice! That was what the classes were for. I'm not going to let him make a bunch of mistakes on my baby and run the risk of hurting him." As if a switch had been flipped on, Teresa's eyes filled with tears. She pulled a tissue from the oversize bear-adorned bag that hung from her shoulder and dabbed at the flood that spilled over onto her face. "Good grief, now he's made me cry again. Sometimes I wonder whether he's worth all the trouble I go through to keep him around."

April and Nicole looked at each other in horror and responded as one. "The baby?"

"Of course not!" Teresa blotted her eyes. She had a baby face herself, with large eyes and round cheeks. Unfortunately, she wasn't as cute as a baby when she cried. Her eyes had become bloodshot, and her nose turned an uncomely shade of red. The young mother honked into the tissue. "I was talking about Will. He's such a doofus when it comes to Liam. Last night he put honey on his pacifier!"

April reluctantly returned the baby to Teresa's outstretched arms. "Lots of people who don't know any better have given honey to their babies. I'm sure a little bit didn't hurt him any."

Teresa looked at her as if she were as untrainable as her husband. "But they told us in prenatal class that babies lack an enzyme that's needed to digest honey. Liam could have gotten sick or ... *died*!"

She burst into renewed tears, and April watched in dumbstruck helplessness as the young woman raged against the ineptitude of her well-meaning husband.

Nicole put an arm around her friend. "Don't you think maybe you're overreacting just a little?"

Teresa lifted her head and wiped away a teardrop that had

fallen onto Liam's chubby arm. "That's what Will keeps telling me. He says I'm having postpartum depression." She fixed her gaze knowingly on them both. "As if he's an expert on having babies. I think he's just trying to shift the blame away from himself."

Nicole patted her arm. "It sounds like he's just trying to help. Why don't you give him a chance?"

"A chance to do what? Inflict permanent damage?" When she didn't get the sympathetic response she wanted, she added, "We keep having fights over the same kinds of things. For instance, I've told him and told him not to put the baby in the swing when he's not sleepy. A couple of days ago, Will did it anyway! When I walked into the room, there was Liam with his eyes crossed because he was trying so hard to focus with the motion of the swing. If he needs glasses in a few years, I'll know exactly why."

"Maybe you need a break," April suggested. The young mom was probably overtired.

"You're right," Teresa agreed. "I need a break from Will. As far as I'm concerned, he can just move back in with his mother."

"No, that's not what I—"

Nicole seemed just as shocked as April by the turn in the conversation. "I think what my aunt meant was that you need a break from the baby. Why don't I come over and babysit tonight while you and Will go out to dinner and a movie? You two need some time alone together."

Teresa shook her head. "We used to fight some before the baby came, but now it's like that's all we ever do anymore. I don't know if it's even worth the effort."

Liam squirmed in his mother's arms and gave a little squeak as if in protest to what Teresa had said. Instinctively, April reached out and stroked his warm head, and he quieted down. She felt inordinately pleased by the way he responded to her touch.

"Sometimes, when you've had a big change in your life," April said, "it's easy to get confused. And that's when you need to go back to the basics."

"You mean that I should move back home with *my* mother?"

"No," April hastened to assure her. "I meant that you should ask yourself how you feel about Will."

"I feel like he's just one big screwup right now," Teresa said emphatically.

April probably should just shut up. She wasn't a trained counselor. In fact, she'd already managed to make things worse, all quite by accident. But she couldn't seem to stop herself. "Do you love him?" she prompted.

Teresa's pause was long enough to make April worry that the answer might be no. Finally, the new mother nodded yes.

"And does he love you?"

Teresa nodded again.

"I'll bet he'd do anything to make sure you and the baby are happy and healthy. Wouldn't he?"

Another nod.

"Then you should be together." She gave Liam's head another stroke. "Besides, the baby needs *both* of you."

Nicole wrote down her telephone number and gave the slip of paper to her friend with instructions to call whenever she needed a babysitter. And they agreed that they would take turns sitting for each other after Nicole's baby was born.

As for April, her own words were still ringing in her ears long after she returned home from her outing with Nicole.

"I'm such a hypocrite," she declared. Colton was at the campground taking care of a jammed cash register, so there was no one home to hear her except Maybelline. And the dog was currently occupied with carrying Colton's sock from the bedroom to the dog bed in the living room.

"Give me that." When Maybelline relinquished her grip on the sock, April tossed it into the hamper where it belonged.

The sock on the floor was evidence that Colton wasn't perfect. But neither was she. She snored. He told her so, and then he laughed about it, saying it made him feel like he was camping out … in a bear's cave. And she folded the towels in halves before hanging them over the rod even though—as Colton had pointed out—they looked neater when folded in thirds. But rather than make a fuss over it, he straightened her towel when she wasn't looking.

Yes, she was a hypocrite. The very things she'd asked Teresa could have been asked of her.

Did she love Colton? As Teresa had done, April paused a long moment. As crazy as it might seem and regardless of how much she tried to deny it, she knew the answer was an unequivocal yes.

And the thought frightened her. All these years Colton had been her best friend. Her comrade. Her ally. Her protector. And ever since her divorce from Eddie, she'd insisted that she and Colton remain "just friends" in order to avoid having a romance ruin their long-standing friendship.

For the first time, April admitted the truth to herself. It was romance that ruined her friendship with Eddie, all right. Problem was, the romantic feelings were the ones she had always harbored for her "best buddy."

At that thought she sat—no, collapsed—on the sofa. She had married the wrong man. That was why the marriage hadn't worked.

They'd been a threesome during high school; all of them best friends. Eddie had idolized Colton and tried to be like him. If Colton played baseball, so did Eddie, and he tried to outdo him on the diamond. If Colton dressed a certain way, Eddie was certain to show up a few days later wearing similar but better clothes.

When Colton had gone away to college, she had naturally turned to Eddie to help fill the void that their friend had left in their hearts. She could see now that the more she had talked about how much she missed Colton, the harder Eddie had worked to sweep her off her feet. At the time, it had seemed that they had naturally turned to each other to fill the emptiness that Colton had left behind. With the clear focus that accompanies hindsight, April now saw that Eddie hadn't idolized Colton as she'd first thought ... he'd *envied* him. And his competitiveness had led him to pursue her and eventually marry her.

At the time she may not have recognized that she'd been in love with Colton, but Eddie certainly had. Colton might have taken home the high school wrestling trophy, but *she* had been Eddie's trophy. No wonder their marriage hadn't worked. No wonder their friendship had turned so sour.

April sighed. Maybelline's ears lifted at the sound, and the big dog disobeyed the long-standing rule of staying off the furniture. April didn't bother to reprimand the sympathetic retriever as it climbed up beside her and rested its muzzle on her shoulder. She patted her golden-haired friend, and they both sat facing straight ahead, looking for all the world like they were waiting for a bus.

Her mind flitted back to the next question she had asked Teresa that morning. *Does he love you?*

There was no question that he loved her. What she really needed to know was *how* he loved her. Like a sister? Possibly. Like a lifelong best friend? Definitely. Like a wife?

Hmm. April stroked her chin while she considered, and Maybelline breathed on her neck, watching to see if perhaps she was sneaking a bite of candy without offering to share.

There was no doubt that he had *physically* loved her as a man would love his wife. Unfortunately, that didn't tell her anything other than that he had needs, just as she did.

He'd made it clear when he offered to marry her—and again the day of the wedding—that this was a marriage of convenience. He needed her at the campground. Colton was a savvy businessman, but not every owner would make such a personal sacrifice for his business.

Could it be that he was as blind to his love as she had been to hers? True, he had offered to marry her in an effort to hold on to the successful fruits of their campground labors. But if, during the course of their marriage-for-show, he came to see how much he truly loved her, what would be the harm in foregoing the divorce? Their marriage of convenience could grow into a marriage of love and passion.

Which led her to the next question. *Would he do anything to make sure she and the baby were healthy and happy?* Absolutely. There'd never been any doubt in her mind that he would always be there for her, married or not. And the same was true for the baby, whether it was genetically his or an anonymous donor's.

She thought back to the advice she had given Teresa. *You should be together,* she'd said with assurance. *Besides, the baby needs* both *of you.*

It had been so easy to see this truth in Teresa's case. Why had it taken her so long to realize the same for herself?

Sure, April could raise the baby alone. A lot of single women did so and were quite successful at it. But in this case, there was a man in the picture ... a man whom she loved very much. A man who would make the world's best dad.

It was one thing to be a single mom because it was necessary or because she had no other choice. However, it was nothing other than sheer foolishness to become a single mom when she already had a perfectly fine husband who was an excellent daddy candidate.

Then it was settled. She just had to find a way to open Colton's eyes to the love they'd always had between them. And she knew exactly how she would do it.

She would seduce him. She would have to show him they weren't just having sex. They weren't just making a baby. They were making *love*.

April threw her arms around the dog's neck and gave her a hug. In return, she endured wet kisses on her chin.

"I love him," she said more to herself than to Maybelline. "Now all I have to do is make him see that he loves me, too."

For the first time since she and Colton had agreed on their baby making plan, she hoped she didn't get pregnant right away. If it happened too soon, a pregnancy could spell the end of their relationship before it even began.

April opened the shed door on the bathhouse roof and took out a speaker hooked up to her playlist and a bag of prizes for the winners of tonight's dance contest. This was one of her favorite events, and the teens—many of whom considered family camping to be uncool—were grateful for the activity that catered to their interests.

It was also for this that she had worked out a standing arrangement with the youth facility that allowed Steven to break his nighttime curfew. Although her main purpose in having him stay each Friday night was to allow him time to socialize in return for his hard work during the week, she had convinced the youth facility administrators that she needed the boy's help. And though she wanted him to just relax and have a good time, Steven always insisted on helping her, as he did now.

"Hey, what's this?" he asked, pulling out a large box from the back of the shelf and setting it with the rest of the stuff.

"Oh, don't bring that out. It's just some junk that the former owner left behind."

"Man, these are the biggest CDs I've ever seen." Steven held up one of the cardboard covers and withdrew a slightly warped record album. "Who are Tommy Dorsey and Glenn Miller?"

She set down the bag she'd been about to put in the shed and walked over to examine his find. There were records of big band and folk artists from the nineteen-twenties, -thirties, and -forties. And although some of the covers were faded or layered with dust and mildew, the albums themselves were in pretty good shape.

The nostalgic sight brought back memories of time spent at Grandma Hanson's house when April was young. Her grandmother owned what was at the time a new record player but, with a little cajoling from April, would crank up the old Victrola and play the songs that had been old-fashioned even thirty years ago.

"Wow, I haven't heard these in years," April said, remembering afternoon naps on top of the Hanson family quilt while listening to the scratchy tunes of "My Gal Sal" and "Indian Love Song." She turned over one of the albums in her hands and examined the photo of the well-dressed man. "Glenn Miller did a lot of big band music in the forties."

"Gee, I didn't know you were that old." Steven jumped away when she feigned a motion to give him an affectionate swat.

She sent him down to the camp store to get some Japanese lanterns to hang from the rooftop rails. While he was gone, April shoved the bagful of things she'd bought after her revelation last night into the shed and locked the door.

There were scented candles, the white negligee that she

hadn't worn since their wedding night, and a small cooler containing a bottle of champagne and fresh strawberries. She was trying to remember if there'd been anything else she should have brought with her when Colton interrupted her train of thought.

"Guess who I found downstairs?" he announced, stepping aside to make a flourish toward her cousin.

Ardath giggled and moved closer, stubbing her toe against the box of old records.

In her haste to hide the tools of her seduction, April had forgotten to put the ancient music away. Rather than open the shed again and risk having Ardath or Colton find her secret stash, she pushed the box to the corner and made a mental note to put it away later. "Sorry about that," she apologized.

Ardath shrugged it off. "You left your earrings at Nicole's house yesterday. Since I was coming by this way to go home, I offered to drop them off."

"Thanks, but you didn't need to go to the bother." April took the dangly ornaments from her cousin. Normally she wore button-shaped earrings because they were more suited to the type of work she did, but yesterday she'd wanted to wear something a bit more feminine and frilly. However, she'd found the way they swung against her neck distracting and had laid them on Nicole's coffee table.

The pearl and gold shoulder dusters would look pretty with her white nightie. Tonight, nothing could distract her from her planned seduction. She dropped the earrings into her shorts pocket for later.

"I've asked Ardath to stay and do the Electric Slide with us once the dancing begins," Colton said.

"Yes, please stay." April made a little grimace. "But we might not do the Electric Slide. Most of the teenagers prefer the newer dances."

Ardath happily accepted their invitation and helped them string lights. A few minutes later, Steven's voice could be heard on the loudspeaker, informing all teenagers that the dance contests would soon begin.

Though it took some coordination and muscle, Colton and Steven brought Clyde and his wheelchair out onto the bathhouse deck where he performed his duties as disc jockey. The mix of music was eclectic, to say the least. Rap, folk ballads, oldies rock and roll, some country western, modern alternative rock, merengue. A little of this and a little of that. There was something for every teenage taste, and Clyde frequently spoke into the microphone, inter-jecting well-received jokes and teasing comments about the dancers.

When the fun began, April tried to urge Colton out onto the dance floor for a fast number, but he refused, saying he was too tired. Rather than become discouraged by his apparent lack of interest, she tried again a few dances later when the tempo had slowed considerably.

This time he hesitated but didn't refuse. It was obvious, though, that he wasn't thrilled about the idea of dancing with her. Despite his lackluster attitude, he held her tight, and April welcomed the closeness. It was warm out, but from their second-story altitude, the night breeze caressed their bare arms and legs.

She inhaled his freshly showered male scent and was over-come with the urge to kiss him, long and hard. But a glance to her right showed Steven watching them as they swayed to the romantic tune. The thought of kissing Colton was tempting, but there would be plenty of time for that later. For now, however, she focused on teasing him out of his blue mood.

"It's only nine thirty," she murmured near his ear. "If you're this tired so early, maybe I should have set my sights on a younger stud." She slanted a wicked grin up at her husband. "I hear nineteen-year-old boys are at their sexual prime."

He stiffened and pulled her closer. "You don't want a mere boy," he declared. "Besides, I'm always primed."

There was no doubt about that. He was a man of lusty appetites. All April had to do now was convince him that he wanted more than a tryst and a temporary marriage with her. She had to show him that he wanted *forever*.

The door that led downstairs opened, shining a beacon of light across the dance floor. April squinted against the sudden brightness and barely made out the shadowed outline of someone helping another up the last step.

"Oh, no," Colton moaned. "It's the dynamic duo."

❧ 10 ❧

The door swung shut, blanketing them once again in the soothing softness of the muted lamplight. Sure enough, Mrs. Turner and the deputy were making their way across the dance floor toward them.

"Sentimental Journey" ended, and a frenzied song followed. Squinting through the dim light, April could see Steven had commandeered the speaker and bumped the decibel level up another couple of notches. He'd obviously taken notice of their visitors, and this was his way of showing his displeasure.

She followed Colton to the bench that lined the rail and pulled up a more comfortable chair for the older woman who grumpily accepted.

Mrs. Turner had to shout to be heard above the din. "I thought that boy had a curfew," she said, pointing to Steven.

"The headmaster at the youth facility gave him permission to stay late because of his good behavior." April didn't want to dredge up the problems with Steven again, and it was all she could do to keep the sarcasm out of her voice.

"Good behavior? Bah!" Mrs. Turner leaned forward in her

chair and pointed a finger at April and Colton while the deputy gave them a smug grin. "That little delinquent took my crafting supplies and my late husband's tools. And, lest you forget, he set fire to my roses."

Turning to the deputy, the older woman added, "A fine state this world is in when you call that good behavior. That kid ought to be locked up, if you ask me."

April had heard enough character bashing of her young employee. Although the cause of the fire was still uncertain and the disappearance of their neighbor's belongings couldn't be explained away, harsh accusations were not the way to resolve the situation.

"Well, nobody asked—"

Colton silenced her retort by placing an arm around her shoulders and giving her a light pinch. "So, is this what you came to see us about?"

Apparently curious as to why they were being visited by a law enforcement official, April's cousin sidled over to listen in on their conversation.

That's when Dugg stepped forward. April could have sworn he puffed out his chest and sucked in his stomach. "I received notification that noise from your party could be heard on the adjoining property," he said in his most official voice.

April had no doubt who had "notified" him.

"An investigation into the matter revealed that the music—"

"The noise," Mrs. Turner corrected. Her chin bobbed as she nodded self-righteously.

"Yes, uh, the noise can indeed be heard from the Turner property, which makes it difficult for her to sleep."

Even at the ear-splitting level Steven had raised the music to in honor of their unexpected guests, April suspected it could barely be heard over the crickets and cicadas in Mrs. Turner's yard.

Colton caught Steven's eye and signaled him to turn the volume down to a more acceptable level. "The music will be turned off at eleven o'clock," he assured their cranky neighbor.

"Music!" Mrs. Turner harrumphed. "In my day, dogs were put out of their misery for making that kind of noise."

Unable to suppress a giggle, Ardath's mirth came out in an unladylike snort. "Oops, pardon me," she said, directing her comment to Dugg. She daintily raised a hand to her mouth to hide her embarrassment. "I'm just a little jittery from the coffee I drank earlier."

"Jittery," April declared. That was it! "Stay there," she told Mrs. Turner, "I'll be right back."

The heat of their gazes upon her, April retrieved the box she and Steven had pulled from the shed earlier. Colton helped her carry it to the bench. When she removed the albums from the top, she was pleased to find a small electric record player similar to the one that had once stood in the corner of Grandma Hanson's guest room.

Ardath found the cord and plugged it in for her. "April, if the kids think the Electric Slide is fogey music, what makes you think they'll like this junk?"

"Junk!" Mrs. Turner reached for the stack of records. "These were songs to fall in love by."

The local girl Steven had been dancing with joined the ever-widening circle around them. "'Three Little Fish.' 'Dig You Later.' 'A Hubba Hubba Hubba.' What a hoot."

"Don't knock it till you've tried it," the elderly woman admonished.

April swallowed hard. It was a risk, but she had to try *something*. Perhaps a simple gesture would help heal the rift that had grown between them. If not, then at least she would have tried. "What kind of dances did you do when you were these kids' age?" she asked. "Would you show us?"

She didn't have to ask twice. Clyde shut off the boom box and joined the crowd of onlookers who watched Mrs. Turner hike up her jersey knit skirt to show them the fast-paced jitterbug.

At first, some of the kids laughed. But soon even the last holdouts—including Steven—were trying the jitterbug and the mambo. More amusing was watching Ardath and the deputy pair up to try a little bebop.

Ordinarily, Colton would have launched into this unexpected activity with unrivaled enthusiasm. But tonight, he seemed distracted. It felt as though he was trying to distance himself from April when she tugged his hand and urged him to the dance floor. She consoled herself by remembering that he was probably trying to fight his true feelings, just as she had done for so many years.

As the last note faded from the record player, April noticed that the teenagers' initial laughter of derision had now changed to the soul-stirring laughter of joy. She grinned, pleased that her impulsive gesture seemed to have provided them a common bond of friendship.

Mrs. Turner gave a smug smile to the young people around her. "As I said, don't knock it until you've tried it."

"You're right, Mrs. T. You shouldn't knock other people's music until you've tried it." Steven's hands were on his hips in an apparent face-off. "Now it's your turn to try *our* dances."

"Oh, no, it's all blowing up in my face," April moaned to Colton.

He pushed his hat back on his head and rubbed the tension away from his forehead. "Steven," he said, the single word a warning in itself.

"He's right, Mrs. T," insisted the sweet young thing Steven

had been dancing with. "I bet you'd be surprised at how much your dances are like ours."

It was obvious their neighbor didn't believe that for a minute.

"No, really. Watch." The speaker blared again, and this time the girl danced the butterfly to a modern tune. "See, it's sort of like the Charleston, only you don't cross your hands over your knees. You just move them gracefully in and out, like butterfly wings."

Mrs. Turner followed suit, but the flaps under her arms made them look more like bat wings. Once she'd perfected that dance, the teens then moved on to the floss, which they likened to the twist.

"Better watch out," Colton warned April, "or the next thing you know they'll be sharing makeup tips and giggling on the phone with her."

She watched, pleased beyond measure, as her elderly neighbor tried the various steps that the young campers and local kids taught her. This was the second time she'd seen Mrs. Turner smile, and it was a welcome sight.

As for the deputy, he seemed to have forgotten all about the noise level that he'd come to complain about. It was as if Ardath had cast a magic spell on him, turning him from a greasy schmuck into a pleasant little guy whose awkwardly funny gyrations made the pistol bounce at his hip.

The magic also seemed to envelop Ardath. It was probably only the halo from the electric company several miles away, but a kind of glow appeared around her. Usually, her cousin became self-conscious in large groups, but tonight it looked as though nothing could shake her confidence. She was a woman who'd hooked a man's attention, and she was giddy with power.

April looked up into the black sky and fixed her gaze on a bright star. Although it wasn't the first star of the night, she wished anyway. Wished for the magic that surrounded Ardath and the deputy to touch her and Colton.

"How about something slow now?" Colton suggested.

While the young people bickered over which song to play, Mrs. Turner pulled out a record and placed it on the player. The sweet, romantic strains of a waltz filled the night. When the teens complained that they didn't know how to dance to it, she offered to teach them. Unfortunately, neither Colton nor Alexander knew the steps, either.

Clyde rolled his chair to the center of the floor and stretched his hand out to Mrs. Turner. "May I?"

To her credit, their dance instructor hesitated no more than a second or two before she accepted his offer. Despite the encumbrance of the wheelchair, the two moved gracefully around the floor. To and fro and circle around. They moved like they'd trained for this dance.

Right in front of them all, something happened to Mrs. Turner. Like the Grinch whose tiny heart grew three sizes, their neighbor transformed. Wearing a smile of demure sweetness that could charm even the hardest of hearts, her gaze did not stray from the face of her partner. As for Clyde, he looked like he'd just seen Miss America in person.

"I think I'm going to be sick," said Colton, and he went and sat down.

After the music died down and they were left alone on the bathhouse rooftop, April was tempted to scold her husband for his rudeness. But, figuring that wasn't the best way to initiate a seduction, she bit her tongue.

By now, the teens had returned to their campsites or, if they were locals, to their homes. In an obvious change of heart, the deputy had offered to take Steven back to the youth facility. April's first impulse had been to decline the offer, but Steven was willing, and he'd assured her and Colton that there were no more hard feelings between them.

There must certainly have been magic at work tonight.

Now, here they were alone together under the starlit sky. It wasn't the first time they'd locked themselves up here away from the rest of the world.

This was a favorite spot for them after a hard day of tending to their campground duties. If they sat on the bench at the rail, they could see most of the campground from up here. The chorus of crickets, the faraway flickers of camp-fires, and the warm, sweet smell of summer entertained her far more than any show on television.

Or, as they more often chose to do, they could lounge on floor cushions, unseen by all but the blinking stars above them. Usually they just talked about the day's events and their plans for the next day, but tonight Colton was in for a surprise.

Mrs. Turner had said the music from her era was the kind that couples fell in love to. Deciding it was worth a try, April set the turntable spinning again and stacked it with "Let Me Call You Sweetheart," "Moon River," and "Til the End of Time." She had the shed open and was reaching for the candles when Colton rattled the knob on the door leading downstairs to the camp store.

"I'll see you at home, April. Hey, why's the door locked?"

She hesitated, wondering how to say, *I'm trying to seduce you*. Instead of saying it outright, she opted for coyness. She'd never thought she would be the kind of woman to bat her eyelashes, but it turned out to be easier than she thought.

"I was hoping you and I could stay and visit for a little while tonight, Colton. In private."

He swung around to face her. "You've never called me Colton before."

She struck a match and held it to a candle. The flame caused shadows to dance across his handsome face. He was frowning, a condition that she would have to change quickly if she wanted to see her goal accomplished.

"No matter what our original agreement had been, we're no longer just 'buddies' anymore," she admitted. "We're husband and wife ... on paper *and* in bed."

Now, if only they could be husband and wife in their hearts.

"Stay with me," she asked, laying a hand on his arm. "Make love with me."

The frown vanished, but now he looked perplexed. "Don't you think it's too chilly to be hanging around out here?"

She lowered her voice, trying to make it sultry. "I'll keep you warm."

It only took him a second to reconsider going home. While he straightened the mat and stretched out on it, April placed the candles on the floor where they'd been dancing earlier. Then, having slipped out of her coverall shorts and into the white gown, she retrieved the strawberries and champagne and poured two glasses of bubbly.

Colton's eyes were closed, and it looked as though he'd fallen asleep. April supposed she could wait another day or two to begin her seduction, but she knew that every day lost was one less day in which to convince him they were meant to be together.

She bit a strawberry in two, savoring the cool, sweet taste of it. Then it occurred to her how she could wake her husband up and keep him awake.

The touch of her lips to his was enough to stir him. "*Mmm*, you taste good," he said, his voice husky and low.

She lay beside him, her weight supported on one elbow, and plucked at the buttons on his shirt.

Colton moaned. "Do you realize what you're doing to me?"

April smiled her response. It must be working. She lowered her head and kissed him again.

He was hot to the touch, and April felt herself growing warmer by the minute. A need so great it hurt circled through her and settled in the lower reaches of her abdomen.

Colton reached for her, pulling her down until she lay atop his scorching body. When he kissed her, his mouth was hot and dry.

Pulling back, April reached for the champagne to moisten his parched lips. When he raised his head, she held the glass to his lips while he took a drink.

In the next instant, April was unceremoniously dumped to the floor as he leapt to his feet.

"Ow, ow, ow," he kept saying over and over, cupping his jaws in both hands. His frantic pacing took him to the bench and back.

"Colton, are you all right?"

He shook his head. "I think I'm dying."

At that, April jumped up and stood in the path of his pacing, forcing him to stop so she could find out what troubled him. "Was it something I did?"

Again, he shook his head. "You know how it feels when you bite into a sour pickle and it 'grabs' you right behind the jaw and under the ears?"

"Yes."

"Imagine that times a thousand."

"Oh, you poor thing." Since he was already bent over and she could reach him, April kissed him on the forehead. Heat emanated from his skin. "You're burning up with fever. Do you hurt anywhere else?"

"My muscles ache, and my head hurts."

He paced back to the bench and sat down. It was unlike

him to voice complaints, so she knew he must be in a great deal of pain. They were not unlike the symptoms her cousin Jasmine had shown shortly after their wedding.

April sat beside Colton. Gently, taking care not to hurt him any more, she stroked her fingertips along both his jaws. The skin was hot and puffy to the touch.

"Oh, no." The words were out before she could censor her reaction.

For a moment, he stopped shivering and frowned at her. "What?"

She tucked her arm around his waist and leaned against him, hoping he wouldn't see the disappointment in her eyes. Hoping that her guess was wrong. Hoping this wouldn't be as serious as she feared.

"I think you have the mumps."

"I don't think you should be out of bed yet," April informed Colton.

"And I don't think you should be hovering over me, telling me what to do."

Immediately, Colton regretted snapping at her. It wasn't her fault he was sick. Or that he got grumpy when forced into inactivity.

Except for brief periods when she filled in at the camp store or handled a problem that one of their regular employees couldn't deal with, she had been with him almost constantly for the past five days.

Judging by the way she'd taken his temperature and filled him with chicken soup, crackers, and ginger ale, she was born to be a mother.

Colton got up from his sickbed and walked over to where April stood staring out at their rural road. Slipping his arms around her waist and tucking his chin against her neck, he thought about what the doctor had told them.

He'd been pretty feverish at the time, so he didn't remember the statistics the doctor quoted. But two words stood out in his memory: *possible sterility.* From that time on, he'd been able to think of little else besides what this new development might do to the tentative bonds he'd established with April.

He kissed her cheek, then regretted doing so when he saw the red mark left by the rasp of his whiskers. "I'm sorry I've been such a grouch," he told her. "I'm just not used to sitting still for such a long time."

He paused a moment, knowing that wasn't all of it. Knowing that she realized there was more. "And I've had a lot on my mind lately."

Just as she must have. He wondered how long it would take her to suggest they end their farce of a marriage now so she could find another father prospect for her baby. For the hundredth time, he recalled her joking comment about finding a younger stud. Sure, she'd said it in a teasing way, but wasn't there at least a drop of truth in all humor?

She turned in his arms and looked up at him, her smile the sweetest he'd ever seen. Or ever wanted to see.

"I know you're fidgety, but the doctor said you should rest for a whole week. So, don't even think of going back to work until this weekend." She stroked the stubble on his chin. "Why don't you see what's on TV? Or maybe we could play another game of Life?"

Life. As if the real thing wasn't enough to boggle their minds. He stepped away from the woman who'd been his wife for such a short time ... and yet had made him the happiest he'd ever been. "I'm going outside to see if the mail has come yet."

She eyed him warily, and he knew what was coming.

"All right," she said, acting like a warden allowing an inmate out for a breath of fresh air. "But I don't want you jumping rope with the Farley twins or skateboarding with Patrick. You're still contagious, you know."

He held up his right hand as he headed for the front door. "I hereby solemnly swear not to infect the neighborhood kids."

Out of habit, he reached for the battered hat that hung on a peg by the door and plunked it on his head. Once outside, he drank in the sweet smell of an impending summer shower and thanked God he didn't have to work in an office. The wild blackberry bush that had grown up near the mailbox bowed under the weight of so many red berries. Two had ripened to a plump black, and Colton popped them into his mouth while he sifted through the mail. Their tangy sweet juice caused him to wince, but he gratefully noted that the pain was less than it had been several days ago.

He retrieved the newspaper from its box and then checked the mail. Phone bill, advertising circular, magazine. And an envelope addressed to April—from the fertility clinic.

The light-headedness that he'd suffered for the past several days returned in full force, and he felt sick to his stomach. Colton knew the symptoms had nothing to do with the mumps and everything to do with the envelope he held in his hand. Turning it over, he saw that the seal wasn't firm.

He debated for a moment. Although he'd never opened her mail without her consent, he felt like this concerned him as much as it did her. Even so, he experienced a twinge of guilt as he lifted two sheets of paper from the envelope.

The cover letter confirmed her appointment for several weeks from now. The attached sheet gave a listing of potential donors. Identification number, height, weight, and hair and eye color. Even their education and careers were listed.

April had everything she needed here for a custom-ordered baby. And none of it included him.

The postmark was Monday, barely three days after he'd come down with the mumps. She obviously hadn't wasted any time adjusting her plans. Too bad she couldn't have been bothered to discuss it with him.

Maybe she thought she was sparing his feelings. After all, most guys would get pretty testy about having their virility questioned.

He refolded the papers and stuffed them back into the envelope, fighting the temptation to ball it all up and toss it into the garbage can. Instead, he resealed the envelope and tucked it under his arm with the rest of the mail.

With a weary heart, Colton knew he couldn't continue this marriage charade any longer. As soon as he got to a phone, he decided, he would call up an old friend of his. Without a doubt, Yvonne could help him through this.

But first he'd have to find his little black book.

The very second Colton was cleared to return to work, he returned to the campground, throwing himself into his work with more zeal than April thought he was ready for. But when she tried to caution him to take it easy at first, he laughed off her concern by saying that she no longer needed to mother him.

Nevertheless, she was trying to get him to sit down for a rest and a cold drink when the bell jangled on the door. April didn't need a doctor to tell her that her blood pressure rose when Alexander Dugg walked into the camp store. She had hoped that the temporary truce they'd established at the dance last week would mean the end of his snooping into their business. But, as usual, he appeared to be looking for something, as though if he searched hard enough, he might find a criminal lurking around the corner.

Today, however, he wasn't dressed for duty. In place of his uniform, he wore new jeans and a crisp, plaid shirt that was buttoned all the way up to the collar. He reeked of aftershave.

Colton flopped onto the pew bench with his back to the deputy and snapped open a soda can. "If you're trying to go undercover, it isn't working," he said, pausing to sip his drink. "We can see through your 'disguise.'"

"I'm not on duty today." Dugg strolled over to the counter. Selecting a package of beef jerky, he handed some cash to April. "I'm looking for someone."

Maybelline strolled over from her napping spot under the window and sat at Dugg's feet in hopes of a handout.

April plunked his change down on the counter. "Why don't you ease up on Steven? He's trying his best to get his life straight."

Dugg took a bite of the jerky. Then, noticing the golden-haired beggar, he tore off a small piece and dropped it. The meat never hit the floor. "I know he is."

Colton sat up straighter on the bench and turned toward them. It was obvious he was as surprised by the deputy's statement as she was.

"We had a long talk on the way back to the youth facility last week," he continued. "He's not a bad kid."

To say April was pleased would have been an understatement. "So, you believe us? You agree he didn't have anything to do with the fire or the missing items?"

Dugg paused as if searching for the right words. "I believe he won't do it again," he said gently.

It wasn't the answer she wanted to hear, but it was better than his previous attitude. "Then why did you come here today?"

The man who stood in front of her, staring down at the

floor and scuffing his toe against the tile, was nothing like the arrogant deputy with the puffed-out chest and even bigger head. He looked almost ... bashful.

"I was wondering if you might give me your cousin's phone number. They're having a bluegrass festival over in Lakewood this evening, and since I'm not working, I thought I'd ask Ardath to do some clogging with me."

April couldn't help staring at the little man. What would he surprise them with next?

"Well, okay," she said, searching for a scrap of paper. "As long as clogging is all you plan to do. Oh, and undo that top button on your shirt."

His face split into a huge smile of relief, and for the first time since she'd met him, April actually thought he looked rather cute.

The door swung open again, and one of their regular campers entered. Only it looked like he had something on his mind other than buying supplies. "I need to talk to you," he said, addressing both April and Colton.

To her chagrin, the deputy loitered and fed the four-footed mooch while Mr. Quesenberry described the items that were missing from his campsite. Odd items with no apparent value.

"I didn't bother to mention it after my wife's hairbrush disappeared because I figured she might have put it down somewhere and forgot about it," he told them. "But then someone took our spark lighter and the metal fitting to our cookstove while we were at the lake, and the man camping beside us told me he was missing a cooking fork."

Colton got up from where he'd been listening to this unfortunate news. "Mr. Quesenberry, we're sorry your things are missing. Why don't you let us replace what was taken? No charge, of course."

The elderly gentleman smoothed back the strand of white

hair that had fallen across his face. "It's not the cost that bothers me. It's the principle."

"Believe me," Colton assured the man, "we're going to find out who's doing this."

When Mr. Quesenberry left the store, April hoped Dugg would go with him. Instead, he stayed behind, acting like he and Maybelline were the best of friends.

"I don't understand why anyone would steal a bunch of useless stuff," she mused.

Dugg cleared his throat. "I hate to say it, but down at the youth facility, they can turn all kinds of junk into weapons."

"A hairbrush?"

The deputy shrugged. "You'd be amazed."

A few hours later, April received a phone call from one of Colton's old girlfriends.

"There's no need for you to disturb him," Yvonne Jackson said. "Just tell him that the bank has approved his loan to refurbish his house. I'll send him a confirmation letter in the mail."

April's hand shook as she hung up the phone. "The Bachelor House," he'd always called it.

With a heavy heart, she reluctantly acknowledged that her temporary husband was anxious to get back to his bachelor life. Unbidden, a memory returned to her of the time she'd asked him why he never settled down and got married. His response—that he enjoyed the chase too much— had been promptly followed by a flirting invitation to go out with him.

She had been fooling herself when she thought she could seduce him into wanting to stay married to her. The love he had for her was obviously the love of one lifelong friend for another. He was a man who enjoyed his freedom, and her wish to make him love her in a romantic sense was a selfish one. He had already given her so much by agreeing to their marriage of convenience and trying to give her the baby she wanted. It wasn't fair of her to ask for more.

Brushing away the tears that threatened to spill from her eyes, she supposed she wasn't the first woman to think she could make him want to be married and start a family together.

It was just as well that she found out now, she decided, for at this point she would not be able to watch him step out of her life if he fathered a baby with her. With a sadness that permeated her soul, she conceded that the longer she stayed married to Colton, the harder it would be to let him go.

Taking a key from the ring at her belt, she opened the box on the wall in the game room and refilled it with tokens. Just like the fake metal coins, their marriage had been an insincere copy of the real thing. She'd used that token marriage in a game she played, and the prize would have been a baby.

But while she'd been playing the game, she had fallen in love with Colton. And while that was happening, the prize had somehow lost its luster.

No matter how much she wanted a baby, she knew it just wouldn't be the same if it wasn't Colton's. Remaining childless, agonizing though it might be, was a less painful option than raising his child without him. Less painful than looking into that child's precious face and being reminded daily of the love that would never be hers.

That evening, Colton seemed surprised by her sudden decision to call off their baby making plan. When he tried to convince her that he was willing to complete their agreement, it took every ounce of courage April possessed to insist that he take back his freedom.

"If it's because of the mumps..."

"No, it's not that."

"I've been given a clean bill of health."

How could she explain this to him when it was so hard for her to accept the reality of it herself?

"All my life, you've come to my rescue," she told him. "On more occasions than I can count, you've bailed me out of trouble, given me a comforting shoulder to lean on, and set aside your own plans in order to take care of me."

She paced the floor while he sat on the bed they had shared until now.

"I've already taken advantage of your good nature more than I should have," she continued. "I can't let you, out of a sense of obligation, continue putting my needs before your own happiness. Let's just call an end to the marriage and get on with the rest of our lives."

Colton stood and tried to take her in his arms, but she wouldn't let him. If she allowed herself to step inside the safe circle of his arms, she would never be able to leave it.

"What about the baby?" he asked. "I thought you wanted a child more than anything else in the world."

Once, that had been true. But now April knew that even a hundred children wouldn't fill the aching void left in her heart.

When she didn't say anything, Colton lifted her chin with his finger, forcing her to gaze up into his pale-brown eyes. "April, honey, I *want* to give you a baby. I want you to be happy."

She could tell he was sincere, proving once again that he was the best friend a person could ever ask for. Unable to face the questions in his eyes, she turned away from him.

"I'm as happy now as I'll ever be," she said in all honesty.

That night Colton didn't sleep at her apartment but returned the next day to collect his things and take them back to his house.

A few days later he launched wholeheartedly into fixing up his bachelor house. In its location off the driveway into the campground, April passed it twice every day going to work and returning home. Unwilling to witness the evidence of Colton's new life without her, she averted her eyes from the construction site. April saw the remodeling as proof that he was happy to go back to his single life.

The same couldn't be said for her. The apartment they had shared, which once rang with laughter, was now depressingly quiet without Colton.

To make matters worse, an awkwardness had settled over them. To avoid the painful stretches of silence, they put distance between them by working in different areas of the campground. When they were required to work side by side, silence echoed in the space that was once filled with lively conversation. And when they did talk, it was about the latest theft.

The tension was enough to make her physically sick.

Although she blamed it on the heat, she knew it was one of the symptoms of a broken heart.

As summer neared its end, April was relieved to hear the fire investigator's report that the blaze behind Mrs. Turner's house had not been deliberately set.

"Spontaneous combustion," he'd said. "Green hay, dry weather, and the sun providing heat, all contributed to the fire. It's a wonder it doesn't happen more often."

It did her heart good to know that Steven had had nothing to do with the fire. But April was baffled by the continuing disappearance of various items. Even the cell phone that she often carried in her back pocket had disappeared.

Until the phone disappeared, the missing objects seemed to be selected randomly, with no thought given to their value or usefulness. The main consistency had been that the missing belongings were all small.

Small enough to be stuffed into a pocket, perhaps? Small enough to be smuggled past a youth facility guardian?

"I told you I didn't set that fire," Steven said the next day as she checked the chemicals in the pool.

April replaced the cover over the filter and stretched the kink out of her back. "Yes, you did," she agreed, "and I'm sorry I doubted you."

"It's okay." He picked up the bucket of pool supplies and

fell into step beside her as they returned to the camp store. "If I was you, I would've thought the same thing."

When they reached the store, however, April didn't go inside. She needed another few moments to talk to Steven in private. Stalling, she opened the vending machine and counted the empty drink slots.

Steven sat on the bench and wrote down the inventory numbers she called out for each flavor. Maybelline joined them and sat on the boy's foot. During the few months he'd been working at Cozy Acres, the pair had become practically inseparable. Whenever he was around, the dog was right beside him, making it clear she thought he could do no wrong.

April hated to bring the subject up, but she hated even more the thought that the thefts would go unsolved and her young employee would carry the burden of suspicion. Swallowing hard, she decided to just come right out and say it.

"You know, Steven, because of your past some people naturally assume you're the one who took the missing stuff."

"Yeah, I know. Once a convict, always a convict." He reached down and scratched the dog's ears. Maybelline might not be bright enough to fetch a newspaper, April noted, but her pet knew how to comfort a lonely boy. "At least Mrs. Turner isn't bugging me anymore."

He was right about that. It was amazing how much their elderly neighbor's attitude had changed since she'd started working at the campground, teaching crafts to youngsters. And whenever Clyde was near, Mrs. T—as she was affectionately called by the young campers—acted almost girlish.

Closing the drink machine door, April locked it and sat on the bench beside the boy. "You were never a convict," she said emphatically. "The trouble you got into was minor, and sending you to the youth facility was an attempt to prevent you from getting into worse situations." Spreading her arms wide, she added, "And look how well it's working. Colton and I couldn't ask for a better employee. We've even come to think of you as part of the Cozy Acres family."

She hadn't thought it possible, but Steven actually blushed.

"I'd like to solve this problem of the stuff disappearing," she continued, "and I especially want to clear your name. If you know anything about it or can give us some suggestions as to what's going on, it would be a great help."

"I know!" He sat forward on the bench and snapped his fingers. "I bet Rocky's been taking the stuff. Remember how he loved to take junk off the counter and stash it under the blanket in his box?"

For a moment April's hopes soared. And then reality kicked in. "No, all he did was swipe some food from a couple of picnic tables."

Steven laughed at the memory. "Yeah, he just sat down and helped himself while that family from Georgia was saying grace. Imagine their shock when they opened their eyes and saw a squirrel eating off their plates."

It had been funny to hear them tell of the crazed squirrel that refused to be shooed away from their picnic. But as much as she wished the rodent could have provided the explanation, she knew he wasn't the answer. "Things started disappearing before we set Rocky free."

He looked crestfallen, and April fought the urge to wrap her arms around the boy and hug him.

"Oh, I forgot about that."

"Don't worry," she assured him with a pat on the knee. "We'll figure it out soon. Let's go inside—this heat is enough to make a person puke."

She was reaching for the pool supplies when Steven stopped her.

"April?"

"Yes."

"I'm real sorry things didn't work out between you and Colton."

"Yeah," she said. "Me, too."

A cicada whirred its wings in the treetop and soon others joined in the chorus, creating a din that matched the unrest in April's spirit.

"What you said about me feeling like a part of the Cozy Acres family," he began with hesitation. "Did you really mean that?"

"Of course I meant it." April leaned against the bench back and studied the boy she had come to care so much about these past few months.

He slouched in response to a growth spurt that had rocketed his height to six feet. As he leaned forward, gently pulling Maybelline's jowls into comical expressions, his brown hair fell across his forehead. Dark specks shadowed his upper lip, giving evidence that it had been several days since he'd shaved away his newly sprouted whiskers.

Without looking up, he opened his mouth to speak, then paused as if he thought better of it. After a shy glance in her direction, he came out with what was on his mind.

"You know, I had this dream one time. It was kinda stupid, actually," he said self-consciously. He lifted Maybelline's ears and flapped them like wings. "I dreamed that you and Colton were still together."

April nodded. She'd had that dream many times herself.

"And I was your kid, and Maybelline slept on my bed." As if embarrassed by admitting his fantasy, he rushed on. "Mrs. T and Clyde were in it, too, and—get this—I was calling them Grandma and Grandpa. As if!"

It didn't take a psychology degree to understand that he wanted exactly what she desired—a family. Having been bounced from one foster family to another, the teen wanted to settle where his roots could grow deep.

Something stirred way down inside her, kicking up long-forgotten memories of wishing for her father to return home so that her own family would be complete. Her dream of a perfect family had not come true—either as a child or as an adult—but she hoped that Steven would someday achieve his dream of a family who would love him and give him a sense of belonging.

She stood and placed a hand on his shoulder. "That's a very sweet thought. I hope that someday you'll have all you wish for."

As for April, the situation was a bit more complicated. Stepping inside, she brushed a hand over her abdomen.

She would soon have what she had wished for ... but not what she hoped for.

~

"I hear congratulations are in order," Colton said as she walked along the brick path in front of his bachelor house.

April almost dropped the housewarming present she'd brought him. "But how did you know?"

He grinned and set the hammer on the post at the base of the steps. "The stable manager told me."

"He did?" She wondered how their employee had heard about the news.

"Yeah, it looks like Daisy's romp in the hay is going to cost us a hefty stud fee."

"Oh, that." She swung her arms, contemplating how best to broach the subject she'd come to discuss. Still at a loss, she satisfied herself with small talk. "The house is looking good."

It was old, but it had a homey feel to it, especially now that Colton had repaired the porch and refreshed the exterior with a new coat of paint. Without his saying so, she knew that he was here to stay. She found no comfort in that knowledge.

"Let me show you the rest," he said, reaching for her hand. "Hey, what's this?"

She shrugged and offered him the brightly wrapped package. "It's just a little something for the house. I thought you could use a little plaque for the door to celebrate its new look."

"You didn't have to," he said needlessly. He placed the package on the wicker chair by the front door and took her hand in his. "Let's open it together after I show you what I've done to the inside."

"Colton, I need to talk to you about something."

He stopped in his tracks but didn't release her hand. Instead, his fingers closed more tightly around hers, and he studied her with a mixture of curiosity and awkwardness. She realized too late her mistake and tried to cover the gaffe by babbling.

"I mean, uh, Buddy." For some reason, the old nickname didn't feel right on her tongue anymore. "We really need to talk before any more time passes."

"If it's about the missing stuff, I don't think Steven did it." He tugged her hand. "Come on."

"Wait."

After Steven had shared his dream with her, she'd been forced to consider whether he may have taken the items to get attention. Even so, she honestly didn't believe he'd had anything to do with the mysterious disappearances. But that was only one of the things she'd come to discuss with Colton.

"It's about the marriage thing that we arranged. We need to figure out what we're going to do next."

"You want a divorce," he said flatly. "Sorry, but I've been

kind of busy with the renovations here. Haven't had time to file the papers."

Before she could tell him what she had on her mind, he was leading her through the house, proudly displaying the new paint and modernized kitchen. "Next, I'm going to knock down that wall to add another room, and I was thinking of converting the side porch to a Florida room."

He gave her a broad smile, the first genuine smile she'd seen on him since they went their separate ways. He stood in the middle of the living room, proudly surveying the changes he'd wrought in the house.

"So, tell me," he said, "what do you think? From a woman's point of view, of course."

A woman's point of view. So that was it. He wanted to know how his female visitors might respond to his love den.

With an aching heart, April recalled his joking comment of a few years ago. When Clyde had teased him about being a wild, carefree bachelor, he'd laughingly told them he was thinking of adding mood lighting and turning his bachelor house into a seduction palace. At the time, she had thought he was only teasing, but now she wasn't so sure.

Looking around her, April soaked up the coziness of the room. It was a house any woman would love. Warm and inviting. The problem was, the invitation didn't have her name on it.

A movement outside the window caught her eye. "What was that?"

"Did you see it, too?"

They both went to the window. Their shoulders bumped companionably as they put their heads together to peer out into the side yard.

"It's just Maybelline," Colton said, not bothering to step away now that he knew what they'd seen. "She probably followed you here."

April leaned closer to the window until her forehead touched the pane. The dog trotted across the yard with something in her mouth. "What do you suppose she has? It's kind of small and gray, and it looks like ... oh, no!" She gasped, unable to speak the word.

Their eyes met, and Colton voiced the thought that struck terror in her heart. "Rocky."

They raced each other to the front door, knocking over a ladderback chair in the process. Since his legs were longer, he was a couple steps ahead of her as they flew down the steps and rounded the corner. Even so, April got there in time to see Maybelline's furry tail disappear under the side porch by way of a broken lattice board that had yet to be replaced.

Colton got down on all fours and peered into the dark hole. April followed suit, calling to her pet to come out from under the house. But Maybelline had other ideas.

After pulling aside the wooden board to make room for his bulky shoulders, Colton went in after the dog.

Out here in the bright sunlight, April couldn't see a thing that was happening under the house. Perhaps it was best that way. Poor little Rocky was such a trusting squirrel. Had he been lulled by his familiarity with the big dog into allowing her too close? April prayed that her little gray friend would survive—for the second time—being caught by Maybelline. She thought she had seen a flash of red on the gray and hoped they weren't too late.

"Quit it," Colton said from under the porch.

April imagined the dog being unwilling to give up the prize she'd found, much as she'd done that first time when Rocky was only a baby. "What's going on in there?"

"Your dog is kissing my ears."

He laughed, and she could hear him moving farther back under the porch. "Do you want me to come in?"

"Only if you're a better kisser than Maybelline is." After

another moment passed, he ordered her to hold out her hands. "Here comes your squirrel."

Something gray was tossed at her, and April moved quickly to catch it. "What do you think you're—"

It was a shoe. A woman's gray orthopedic walking shoe. The distinctive red flash design on the side identified it as belonging to their newest employee.

"This is Mrs. Turner's."

Colton's face appeared at the opening in the lattice and was promptly slurped by a long pink tongue. He wiped his cheek with his sleeve. "Wait'll you see what else is under here."

Out came her cell phone, a small metal pipe from a cook-stove, a long-handled spark lighter, pinecones, and an assort-ment of other junk, including a dozen or more newspapers. Surprise turned to relief as realization dawned on her.

"Here's the last of it," Colton said as he passed her a hammer and a wrench.

"The tools from Mrs. Turner's shed."

"I hate to tell you this," he said with a grin, "but your dog is a kleptomaniac."

And then he handed her the long-missing naked doll that was originally meant to wear Mrs. Turner's crocheted *Gone with the Wind* dress. The plastic form sported a few dents and punctures from sharp canine teeth.

"Looks like you taught her to fetch, after all," he said with a smile. "You must be proud."

April couldn't believe her eyes. "Oh, my gosh. All this time Steven was getting the blame for taking stuff, and Maybelline was the real thief."

At the sound of her name, the golden purloiner stuck her furry face out the lattice opening and grinned at April.

Colton crawled out from under the house and brushed

the dirt off his clothes. "Everything seems to be accounted for."

April was thrilled that Steven was now vindicated. But her joy ended with Colton's next comment.

"There's still one thing of mine that was stolen, and it hasn't been returned," he said ominously. "I know who the thief is, and it's neither Steven nor Maybelline."

She piled the armload of miscellany on the porch and turned back to face her partner. "Do you have any idea who might have done it?"

He nodded solemnly and rested his hands on her arms. "It was you." He must have seen her surprise, for he hurried on with his explanation. "You stole my heart, April."

When she started to protest, he stopped her by taking her into his arms. "It's okay," he assured her, "you don't have to return it. All I ask is that you take the rest of me, too."

She was sorely tempted to let herself melt into his embrace and give in to the lure of his statement. But, although the words rang sweet in her ears, April could not believe them. He must have somehow learned of the main reason behind her visit and was once again putting her needs before his own wishes.

Like a dieter forgoing a delectable slice of chocolate cake, she summoned up all the resistance she could muster. With effort, she even managed to make her tone light and casual.

"Surely you wouldn't want to let this wonderful bachelor house go to waste. Why don't you let me fix you up with a friend of mine? She's pretty and very intelligent."

With her heart throbbing double-time, she waited for him to take her up on her selfless offer. She watched his eyebrows arch upward and steeled herself for his response.

"No matter how pretty or how intelligent your friend is," he said, "she's still not you."

He hugged her tight, and April fought the tears that threatened to spill onto his shirt.

"Come here. I want to show you something." Leading her to the back of the house, he waved a hand toward a large, elaborate play set, complete with sandbox, sliding board, and a make-believe playhouse. "This is not a bachelor house." He turned to her, his brown eyes large and sincere. "It's a family house."

When April flashed him a frown of confusion, he shrugged.

"I may have jumped the gun by putting the swing set up so soon. If the doctor was wrong about the mumps," he reasoned, "we could always adopt. Or, if you want to experience pregnancy firsthand, I'll definitely be there for you when you go for your appointment at the fertility clinic next week."

The tears of heartbreak that had filled her eyes became tears of happiness. Instinctively, her hand went to her belly.

"You don't know," she said, more a statement than a question.

He wasn't aware of her pregnancy, she realized with a sense of elation. All the time he'd been working on the bachelor house, he was actually planning for a future with her and their children. Without a doubt, April knew that he loved her as much as she loved him.

"The clinic appointment was a follow-up from my original visit. I canceled it the day I got the confirmation letter."

Now it was his turn to frown. "But I thought you wanted—"

"It wasn't just a baby I wanted," April said, at long last realizing this truth for herself. "From the start, my desire was to have a *family*. A family I could love and who would love me in return."

A family in which she belonged completely.

April surrendered to the gentle caress of her husband's

lips on hers and happily looked forward to a lifetime of his kisses.

"You know," she said when they came up for air, "even if I weren't carrying your baby right now, I'd have all I ever wanted ... in you."

He stepped away from her, and his gaze dropped from her eyes to her abdomen, which he touched with utmost tenderness. When he looked up at her again, April could have sworn that he glowed with pleasure. "We're going to have a baby?"

She smiled, taking in his excitement and letting it fill her up. With a nod of her head, their lives changed forever.

Colton whisked the hat off his head and hurled it into the air with a whoop of delight. April wrapped her arms around his neck, and he picked her up and carried her over the threshold into their own private love den. The message on the housewarming gift she'd brought—a plaque to hang over the door—now seemed somehow prophetic.

Home Sweet Home.

EPILOGUE

Blue lights flashed in his rearview mirror, and Colton swore under his breath.

"What are you stopping for?" April asked. "We don't have time."

He glanced over at his fidgeting wife, who was trying to make herself comfortable in the passenger seat. Her breathing came in forced, shallow gulps, convincing him her words weren't idly spoken.

"Don't worry. I'll just explain everything to the officer, and we'll get a police escort to the hospital."

His words sounded calmer than he felt inside. With his attention focused on his wife rather than the man approaching their car, Colton responded to the intruder in clipped tones.

"Look, Officer, I know I was speeding, but my wife—"

"It's okay, pal, that's not why I stopped you."

Instantly, Colton recognized Dugg's voice and pivoted to face him. The deputy was already reaching into his pocket. Annoyed at being stopped for something as minor as a burned-out brake light or an expired inspection sticker, Colton gritted his teeth and accepted the paper.

April moaned.

"Or maybe I should call you *Cousin*," Dugg declared, puffing his chest out and smiling for all he was worth. He leaned down so that he could address both of them at once. "Ardath said yes."

Inspecting the paper in his hand, Colton saw that it was an invitation to the wedding. With a glance at the man leaning in his car, he wondered if he himself had grinned that foolishly when April had agreed to stay married to him.

Probably.

"Congratulations," Colton said in the most succinct manner possible. "Look, we've got to—"

"Oh, and there's something else. When I was up at the courthouse earlier today, I heard that the judge has approved your request to become Steven's new foster parents." He clapped a congratulatory hand on Colton's shoulder. "Looks like you're adding one more person to your family today."

April lurched forward in her seat. "Make that *two!*"

Forgetting about the deputy—forgetting about everything but his wife—Colton focused his full attention on the drama unfolding before him. "What is it, honey?"

Her brown eyes met his, her face screwed by pain and impatience. He'd heard that women get like this when on the verge of giving birth.

"What do you *think* it is? It's a baby. And it's coming *now!*"

Once again, she shifted her position and laid a hand on her swollen abdomen.

"Wait here," said Dugg as he headed back to his squad car. "I'll alert the dispatcher for help."

Colton got out of the car. "We don't need help. We need a police escort," he yelled to his future cousin-in-law.

The sound of his own car horn blowing alerted him that they probably wouldn't have time to make it to the hospital. Going around to the passenger side, he saw that April had one foot propped on the dashboard. If she hadn't looked so incredibly pregnant, he would have thought she was just sitting back and enjoying the tentative rays of early spring sunshine.

"It's only twenty minutes to the hospital. Can you wait that long?"

His wife's eyebrows drew together in a plaintive expression, as if the mere thought of waiting any longer would make her cry.

"That's okay, we can do it now if you prefer." He helped her to the back seat.

Dugg returned to his side, holding a blanket and a book. "I've had a little emergency medical training," he told Colton.

"Great, you handle that, and I'll go restart the engine."

"Why?"

"So, I can heat some water on the exhaust manifold."

April suddenly let out a string of language he'd never heard her use before. "Something's happening," she declared, her voice coming out in a wail.

Colton shrugged out of his light jacket and knelt on the dirt shoulder of the road. He took her hand in his. "I'm here for you, honey."

Dugg started unfolding the blanket. "You stay there," he told Colton. "I'll tell you what to do."

The contraction passed, and April relaxed for a moment. "What's the blanket for?"

The deputy held it up between them like a barrier. "So, I don't have to watch."

Another car pulled up behind the deputy's vehicle. Although he'd originally thought the birth of his child was going to be a private affair at the hospital with just him, April, and the medical staff and, of course, the baby, he now welcomed the latest arrival. Hopefully, it would be someone with the volunteer rescue squad.

"Boone Shelton, *Bliss Crier,*" the newcomer announced. "I heard on the scanner that someone's having a baby." The man, big enough to play line back, leaned forward to assess the situation. "Don't mind me. You folks go ahead with whatever you're doing, and I'll just stand over here and take a few pictures."

"Pictures!" April squealed. "Colton, don't let him do it. My hair's a mess!"

She had another contraction, and the newspaperman stepped back to give them their privacy.

Despite Dugg's aversion to watching the miracle that was unfolding before them, Colton was grateful for the instructions the little guy read from the book. But the further along they got in the delivery, the weaker his voice grew.

The early spring air was cool, but April's face glistened with a light sheen of perspiration. She'd never looked more beautiful to Colton, and he told her so. She smiled, and he couldn't remember ever being any happier than this.

Then her face contorted again. "This is it," she announced.

And in the next instant, their daughter slid into his waiting arms. As he cradled her in one arm, they were rewarded with the lusty cries of a healthy infant.

"Congratulations, Mama." Colton thought his chest would burst with pride. "We have a little girl."

"The book says once everything's out, wrap it all up together." Dugg lowered the blanket and peered over at the wet, wriggling bundle. A second later, a thud sounded as the deputy hit the ground. The reporter rushed to attend to him.

Following Dugg's earlier instructions, Colton wrapped the little one in the jacket he'd removed earlier and laid the precious package in his wife's arms. "Let's name her Jewel," he suggested, "because she's our long-awaited treasure."

Her smile told him she agreed. "It's a beautiful name."

"Hey, isn't that the guy who's running for sheriff?" Boone asked.

At their affirmative nods, the camera was aimed at the prone figure on the ground, and the shutter clicked several times in succession.

"Now everyone's happy," April said, cuddling Jewel to her chest. "We got a wonderful new baby, and Dugg is getting the campaign publicity he wanted."

Dear Reader,

Readers are an author's life blood and the stories couldn't happen without you. Thank you so much for reading. If you enjoyed *Colton,* we would so appreciate a review. You have no idea how much it means to us!

To read an excerpt of the first book in Sweet Southern Charmers series, *Reece,* please turn the page.

If you'd like to keep up with latest releases, you can sign up for my newsletter @ https://loriwilde.com/subscribe/

To check out other books, you can visit Lori on the web @ www.loriwilde.com.

Much love and light!

—Lori & Carolyn

EXCERPT: REECE

"Quick, give me your gravy strainer!"

No *hello* or *glad to meet you*. The frantic woman just stood there in Reece's doorway, her hand outstretched in expectation, her dark pageboy hairstyle falling in disarray around her delicate face.

Something resembling a black dog cowered behind her legs ... very attractive legs, at that. Come to think of it, she looked even better close up. Earlier, he'd watched her mow the grass next door from his bedroom window.

He promptly forgot the paperwork he'd been doing and stuck out his hand. "You must be my new neigh—"

"Don't just stand there—we've got lives to save!" The brunette ignored his friendly gesture and pushed past him into the house.

Grabbing his arm, she half dragged him to the kitchen and started digging through his cabinets. The floor grew cluttered with piles of pots and baking pans in her wake.

"Here's a colander." She shoved the thing into his arms. "But the holes are too big. Where's your gravy strainer?"

What was with this woman?

"Umm..." Reece pushed a lock of hair off his forehead. What had he done with that thing after he'd filtered the oil in his tractor?

"How about a flour sifter?" she persisted. When he hesitated to consider what a flour sifter might be, she snapped her fingers under his nose. "Hurry, before they all die!" Reece's clumsy search through the cabinets finally turned up a sifter as well as the misplaced strainer.

"Thanks a million," exclaimed the human hurricane as she slipped out the back door with her bounty. She popped her head back in. "C'mon, I need your help."

It didn't dawn on him to ask why. Even if he tried, he probably couldn't squeeze a word in sideways. Well, what the hell. She had aroused his curiosity. Reece shrugged and jogged barefoot after her across his lawn to her backyard.

He caught up with her at the rail fence and gave her cute bottom a boost across the wood structure. Then he followed her to a small, collapsible pool where she dipped out a bucketful of scummy water.

She set the bucket on the ground and pointed to a hole in the side of the pool. From the hole trickled water and little round black things. On closer inspection, he saw that the black things wriggled in a puddle on the ground.

"My mower tossed a rock through the side of this thing. The tadpoles will die if we don't do something quickly." She held the strainer to the hole and tried to catch the slippery creatures. "Damn—pardon me. This isn't working."

Reece forced his eyes off the sight of her, kneeling in mud and pawing frantically at the flow of water.

"Women," he mumbled and rolled his eyes. "Especial those save-the-whale types."

He pulled off his T-shirt which read, *If You're Not Hungry, Thank A Farmer*, and stuffed it into the hole. He picked up the flour sifter and started scooping out the hapless creatures and transferring them to the bucket.

To his surprise, the woman sat cross-legged, the back of her tie-dyed shorts planted squarely in the mud. She was sure different from hometown women. Obviously a city slicker, but not New York kind of city. No, she didn't seem sophisticated or haughty the way he imagined a metropolitan woman to be. But she was sidewalks and streetlights, apartments and buses.

She seemed unaware of ruining her clothes, she was so intent on capturing, in her bare hands, the tadpoles squirming in the puddle before her.

Not many women he knew would voluntarily touch a live tadpole. Or a dead one, either, for that matter. In fact, he didn't know many girls from Bliss County who'd willingly trade places with the one beside him.

"There." She triumphantly plunged her hands into the bucket and washed the mud and tadpoles from them. "The worst of the crisis is over. Thanks for your help."

Reece couldn't help noticing how the smile reached her greenish-brown eyes even before her lips turned up.

"I'm sorry I acted so rude before. I get carried away sometimes."

He could easily visualize men in white suits hauling her away. Her behavior had been that nutty.

She held out her hand, made a face at the scum and bits of grass clinging to her fingers and large amethyst ring, and wiped the gunk on the front of her shirt. She examined her hand and, satisfied that it was clean enough, stuck it out toward Reece once again. "I'm Lanie, and I just moved in yesterday."

Reece put down the sifter and took her hand in his. Although her bone structure was small, almost fragile, she gripped his hand firmly.

"My name's Reece." He let his eyes wander over her lush figure and noticed she was studying his bare chest just as thoroughly. "Welcome to Bliss." Indeed, the day was getting more blissful by the minute. She improved the scenery immensely.

Water gurgled in the bucket behind Lanie. Her pet had plunged its muzzle up to its eyeballs in the water and was slurping greedily.

Reece stared. It wasn't a dog after all. In fact, it looked like a tiny, knee-high horse.

"Cripes, Winnie, that's not your water bucket." Lanie let go of Reece's hand and grabbed a handful of mane to pull the animal away. "We're trying to save those critters, and you're *drinking* them!"

"A horse? That little thing's a horse?"

Lanie pointed the young animal in the direction of her house and swatted it on the rump to send it away from her lifesaving mission. But the horse decided, instead, to take a cooling walk in the pool.

"That does it." Lanie stepped into the pool, penny loafers and all, and picked up the horse.

Tiny hooves swung wildly in the horse's struggle to get free as Lanie walked toward the house. But it was no use. Lanie opened her back door and set the animal down, shook her finger at it as she muttered something, and closed the screen door behind her. Its squeaky bleats followed her back to the pool.

Reece shook his head. And he'd thought this was going to be another boring Sunday afternoon. "Are you going to leave him in the house to do you-know-what all over the floor?"

"You're a country boy, aren't you? Don't you know the difference between a filly and a colt?" Lanie knelt and went back to scooping the remaining tadpoles from the pool into the bucket. "Even if you didn't, Winnie is a girl's name, you know. And she's housebroken."

How might someone go about housebreaking a horse, he wondered.

Winnie sounded off again. The tiny animal stood dog-style with its front hooves against the door to get a better view of the goings-on outside.

"I've never heard of anyone keeping a horse in the house." He couldn't resist adding, "She'd probably be happier outdoors, where she belongs."

"Aw, hell—pardon me. You're not gonna start on that, too, are you? Hold this."

Lanie thrust the sifter into his hands and began collapsing the sides of the pool until a makeshift spout formed near Reece. He obediently held the sifter under the spout while she lifted, pouring water and tadpoles out of the pool. He dumped the batch of wriggling amphibians into the bucket, and then they repeated the process.

"I was run out of my apartment because of people with attitudes like yours," Lanie said. Her voice rose as she imitated her scorners. "My, my, dearie, don't you know livestock belong outdoors? This is a residential area, and we don't want any horses around here."

Reece again dumped the contents of the sifter into the bucket. "If you feel that strongly about it, why didn't you stay and fight?"

"*Hmmph*. I read about a woman in California who tried to change her zoning code to allow for a miniature horse. After she spent forty thousand dollars in legal fees, she couldn't afford her mortgage." Lanie lifted the pool higher, running the last of the water through Reece's sifter. "No, thanks. I'd rather move to the country where 'livestock' is allowed."

He stood and hoisted the bucket. "You have every legal right to keep a horse here, but I still think it's a dumb idea to let it stay in the house. I don't even let my cat come inside."

"If your cat is the gray one with the white paws, I wish you *would* keep it in your house. I found evidence of him digging in the mulch around my rosebushes."

The woman was raving, and it was unwise to continue the discussion. She obviously couldn't see logic where her pet was concerned.

"There's a pond across the road," he said. "Let's go set these rascals free."

Lanie opened the screen door to let Winnie out, and both ran to catch up with Reece. "Mrs. Masardi's car isn't here," she said as they trudged across the neighbor's property. "Do you think she'll mind if we dump tadpoles in her pond? I met her while moving in yesterday, but I don't know her well enough to help myself to her pond."

"Don't worry, she won't mind." He knew she was almost as nuts as Lanie, except for allowing animals in the house.

Reece was certain their neighbor would gladly give the creatures a home, as long as she didn't have to share her house with them. But would the increased tadpole population attract snakes? He was preparing to give the bucket the old heave-ho when Lanie stopped him with a hand on his arm.

"Don't you dare fling those poor animals into that pond! Give me that."

She took the pail from his hands and waded knee-deep into the water. She lowered the container into the water and let the pollywogs drift out into their new home.

In a squeaky voice, as an adult speaks to a small child, she said, "Come on, you poor little things. Get those tails moving." She gently swished the water with her fingers, then looked up at Reece. "I think they are in shock."

Reece thought that might explain his own condition. Ever since she'd pounded on his door twenty minutes ago, his brain seemed to move in slow motion.

She bent over to speak to the creatures, and her scoop-neck top dangled loosely from her body. His brain—and hormones—suddenly shifted into overdrive.

Have mercy!

At that, Reece did what any red-blooded Southern gentleman in his position would do. He let his eyes linger ever so briefly and drank in the sight of her feminine curves. For one brief, insane moment, he thought about asking her out.

But, no, this woman and her craziness would be bound to upset his life, his mind, and his rigidly enforced work sched-ule. He wouldn't let a pretty face and shapely figure jeopar-dize his two-year struggle to rebuild his family's business.

Irritated with himself for letting her distract him from the week's sales receipts, he snapped, "I don't have time to stand here fooling with a bunch of tadpoles. If they're not moving by now, they're probably dead."

Trying not to notice the hurt expression on her face, he spun on his heel and stalked back to the house.

ABOUT THE AUTHORS

Carolyn Greene

On Carolyn Greene's second-grade report card, her teacher commented, "Carolyn writes nice stories." Shortly after that, Carolyn got hit in the head with a kickball which she credits for her ability to take her romance novels and cozy mysteries in unexpected directions. Over the years, she has been nominated for, or won, numerous writing awards.

Carolyn met Lori Wilde through an online writing forum more than twenty years ago, and they immediately bonded over their mutual love of romantic comedy. Since then, they've brainstormed dozens of novels together and shared a close friendship.

Carolyn lives in Virginia with her hot firefighter husband and two amusing miniature pinschers. They have two grown children and two grandchildren who give her plenty to write about.

Lori Wilde

Lori Wilde is the New York Times, USA Today and Publishers' Weekly bestselling author of 87 works of romantic fiction. She's a three time Romance Writers' of America RITA finalist and has four times been nominated for Romantic Times Readers' Choice Award. She has won numerous other awards as well.

Her books have been translated into 26 languages, with more than four million copies of her books sold worldwide.

Her breakout novel, *The First Love Cookie Club*, has been optioned for a TV movie.

Lori is a registered nurse with a BSN from Texas Christian University. She holds a certificate in forensics, and is also a certified yoga instructor.

A fifth generation Texan, Lori lives with her husband, Bill, in the Cutting Horse Capital of the World; where they run Epiphany Orchards, a writing/creativity retreat for the care and enrichment of the artistic soul.

Made in the USA
Monee, IL
05 July 2021